NIKKI POWERGLOVES

And the Power Trappers

David Estes

This book is dedicated to my dad, who shares my name,
for always being there for me
no matter what new interest I pursue. Your generosity
and love have helped shape who I am today.

Adventures

1	Stakeout	6
2	The Flying Chainsaw Chipmunk	12
3	It's raining Weebles, hallelujah!	16
4	Who's a better dancer: Nikki or a Weeble named Bo Diddy?	20
5	Spencer's big plunger idea	23
6	Who is Nikki's dad?	32
7	The Power Trappers!	41
8	Nikki's second power games	46
9	The funky chicken	54
10	The Great Weeble comes forward	66
11	Gnomes: more than just good gardeners	76
12	Into the Power Trappers' lair	84
13	Finding Axel	89
14	Dart guns: better than laser pistols	97
15	Another power kid, no Samantha	101
16	The third golden door	104
17	The Power Trappers' final trap	107
18	Home sweet home	114
19	A message from the Power Giver	117
Hero	Hero/Villain Cards	120

1

Stakeout

They had done their research. Well, mostly Spencer, Nikki's sidekick, had done the research. He knew everything that had ever been said about STING in newspapers or magazines or on TV. Which wasn't much. Apparently STING was a very mysterious organization. No one really seemed to know what they did. STING stood for the Superior Technology & Information Needs Group. From what Spencer had told her, Nikki knew it was a government agency that had been linked to the disappearance of at least two power kids.

And that was important. Because Nikki's friend had been kidnapped. And her friend was a power kid, too. Nikki had only met Samantha Powerbelts a week earlier, but already they were close friends. Nikki would do anything to help her. And now Samantha needed Nikki's help.

Nikki and her other friends, who called themselves the Power Council, had made plans to get Samantha back. They didn't know for sure who had kidnapped her, but their biggest suspect was STING.

Nikki and Spencer were on a stakeout, which meant they were watching and waiting. Watching the building where STING was located. Waiting for something to happen...or someone to come out...or something. So far they had been watching and waiting for an hour and nothing had happened. Not a single door or window had opened; not a noise had been made; not even a strange smell had wafted from the building. Thinking back, Nikki couldn't even remember a bird flying past the building.

When Nikki and Spencer had first begun the stakeout, she had felt like a spy. Spencer was wearing his dark sunglasses, dark pants, and the dark shirt that said *Boy Genius* on the front. Even though an hour had passed without event, he was flashing his toothy, braces-filled smile. He seemed to be loving every minute of the stakeout even though nothing was happening. But Nikki was getting bored.

Nikki looked up at the clear, sunny sky. There wasn't even a lonely cloud passing by to catch her attention. If there was a cloud, at least she could try and see pictures in it. Like maybe the fluffy, white pillow would look like a grizzly bear. Or a scarecrow. Or something else funny, like a clown or a singing hamster...

Instead, there was nothing in the sky except the sun. Which was pretty typical for summer in Cragglyville. It was hot and dry. Despite the heat, Nikki wasn't sweating. They were hiding across the street from the STING building. No one could see them, Nikki was sure of it. Because they were high in the uppermost branches of a tree, and Nikki was invisible. Spencer wasn't, but his dark clothes would make him hard to spot from the street. Plus, no one was looking at the top of the tree. Why would they?

Nikki glanced down at the gloves she was wearing. She couldn't see them, because they were invisible, just like her. But she could picture them in her mind. They weren't winter gloves, like the kind you would wear while playing in the snow, warm and soft and lumpy. Rather, her gloves were smooth and rubbery, like the kind her mom might use when cleaning the bathroom. One was blue. It had a picture of a bird on it. It had helped her and Spencer get to the top of the tree. Because when she was wearing the blue, bird glove, she was able to fly! And Nikki was good at flying. It was almost as if she had been born to fly.

The second glove didn't match the first. It was gray, with no picture on it. It was her invisibility glove, and when she wore it no one could see her. She couldn't even see herself. She had ten other pairs of gloves, too, but they were tucked away safely inside her magical treasure chest. Each glove gave her a different power.

While Nikki was thinking about her gloves, Spencer whispered, "Look! Something's happening."

Nikki's head jerked to the side so she could see the STING building again. Although the building was still quiet, Spencer was right, something *was* happening. From high in the tree, they could see the roof of the building, which was shaped like a giant dome, smooth and round. A hole had opened in the dome and was getting wider. If she wasn't looking right at it, she might not even notice it. Nikki was glad she had Spencer to help her with these kinds of things. He was good at stakeouts. He was a good sidekick, too. The best.

They watched as the hole in the roof got bigger and bigger. Nikki was tempted to fly over and slip through the hole. She was invisible, after all. No one would see her. She really wanted to know what was in that building. What was STING hiding?

As if sensing what she wanted to do, Spencer reached out and held Nikki's arm. "Wait, Eager-Beaver. Be patient," he said. Nikki's invisible lips curled into an invisible smile. She had no idea how he had read her mind. Or how he had grabbed her invisible arm.

She turned her attention back to the STING building. The dome was completely gone now, having slid back to reveal an open, circular roof. On the roof was a helicopter. But not just any helicopter. It was huge and black and looked dangerous. Mounted on the sides were giant spotlights. Its silver blades were starting to spin—they looked sharp and powerful.

"The lights!" Spencer hissed. "Remember the lights?"

Nikki remembered alright. On the night that Samantha was kidnapped, there was a loud noise from above, and then bright lights had blinded them. It had to be the helicopter! When the lights went out, Samantha was gone.

"They've got her," Nikki said.

Spencer nodded seriously. "Should we try to get inside the building?" he asked.

"I don't think so," Nikki said. "I think we should follow the helicopter. What if they're going to go capture another power kid? We have to try to save them."

Spencer's eyes lit up. "Wickety wickety woo woo!" he exclaimed.

Nikki giggled. She never got tired of Spencer's funny sayings and noises. In this case she knew what Spencer meant. He agreed with her.

The helicopter's blades were spinning so fast that Nikki could barely see them. The sound of the engine was so loud that Nikki had to put her hands over her ears. With a slight lurch, the helicopter lifted off the roof and angled away from the building. Nikki tried to locate the pilot but the glass cockpit was tinted black. The pilot could see out, but she couldn't see in.

She watched as the helicopter sped away from them, away from Cragglyville. "They're getting away, honk honk!" Spencer yelled.

"Nothing can fly faster than me!" Nikki yelled back. "Hop on, sidekick!"

Spencer grinned and then patted at the air to try to locate Nikki's invisible body. She reached and grabbed his hand and pulled it to her shoulder. Spencer climbed onto her back and yelled, "All systems go, Captain-Kangaroo!"

Nikki took off like a rocket.

In seconds she was high above the earth. Everything looked miniature, like the world was just a bunch of toys. The big trees in the forests surrounding Cragglyville were as small as weeds. The automobiles lining the streets looked like Matchbox cars. The people were tiny, like the Lilliputians from *Gulliver's Travels*. Nikki knew that nothing had really gotten smaller, but just looked that way because she was so high up.

As she flew, she was careful to steer well away from a big jet airliner that was carrying passengers across the country. Even though she knew she could outrun the plane if she had to, she didn't want to frighten the pilot by suddenly appearing outside of his window.

Nikki kept the helicopter in her sights, but didn't get too close, as she didn't want them to know they were being followed. They flew together for a long time—the helicopter in front and Nikki and Spencer trailing behind. Finally, the helicopter slowed.

A big, gray shape appeared on the horizon. "Is that...?" Nikki said, trailing off.

"It is!" Spencer said, reading her mind again. "It's Phantom's Peak!"

Nikki hadn't really been paying attention to what direction they were flying, but now she realized that the entire time they had been heading for her favorite mountain. Phantom's Peak was the location of the secret hideout used by the Power Council. Inside the mountain was an amazing place called the Power City. It's also where Nikki and Spencer had first met Samantha Powergloves and the rest of the good power kids and their sidekicks.

And the helicopter was heading right for the mountain! As they approached, gray clouds swirled around the peak, making it look as if there were giant ghosts haunting the jagged cliffs.

"They've discovered the Power City!" Nikki exclaimed.

"Maybe not," Spencer said. "They might go right past it."

Nikki knew he was right but wasn't about to take that chance. The rest of the Power Council was inside the Power City, waiting for Nikki and Spencer to return from their stakeout of STING headquarters. If the people in the STING helicopter found them, they would try to kidnap them, just like Samantha. She had to do something!

With a burst of speed, Nikki took off toward the helicopter, which was getting closer and closer to the mountain. As she flew, she pried off her gray invisibility glove and shoved it into her pocket. Suddenly she could see her hands and arms again. "Welcome back," Spencer said.

"Thanks," Nikki mumbled. She was concentrating on the helicopter. If she got too close to the blades, they would cut her to bits. Spencer, too. So she dropped her altitude and came up from below the flying vehicle, where the landing gear was.

When she got close enough, she grabbed one of the landing skids and pulled herself up. Spencer was still on her back, hanging on for dear life. For once she wished he wasn't with her—for his own safety. From back to front, she tiptoed along a shelf on the side of the helicopter, until she was next to the tinted window. She reached up and rapped hard on the glass. *Crack, crack, crack!*

The helicopter swerved, but it didn't matter. Nikki was already gone. She had leapt into the air and was speeding away. She outstretched her arms and tried to gain speed. She heard the helicopter engine roar. It was chasing her!

2

The Flying Chainsaw Chipmunk

The wind rushed through Nikki's hair. Spencer yelled, "Faster! Faster!"

Nikki knew the helicopter was gaining on them, but that was okay. If she escaped too easily, the STING team might go back to the mountain. She didn't want that. She needed to lead them far, far away.

Nikki twisted her head to look back. The sleek, black helicopter was whirring and churning behind her, like an evil monster tearing through the sky, searching for children to eat. And it especially liked kids with powers, like Nikki. But she wasn't worried, or scared. Because she had a trick up her sleeve. One that would guarantee her escape from the flying hunk of metal.

When the helicopter got close, she dove for the ground. The copter dipped, chasing after her. It was remarkably agile for such a large vehicle. When it dipped, however, she cut sharply to the left, circling around behind it. Nikki thought for sure that the pilot would be confused, unsure of how to pursue her.

Instead, to her amazement, the copter stopped instantly, and then swung around to face her. The tinted black window looked like a giant eye, staring at her and Spencer, gleaming in the sun. Nikki expected the pilot to propel the copter toward her again. But he didn't.

With an awkward lurch, the helicopter swept to the side, facing a different direction and leaving its side door angled toward Nikki.

The door slid open.

A man wearing dark green army pants and a dark gray tank top peered out. She couldn't see his face because he wore a helmet with a dark visor. He was huge. His arms were like steel poles, bulging with rock hard muscles. His chest was the size of a boulder and looked like bullets would bounce off of it. He was Superman, except bigger, and stronger.

Then Nikki noticed his gun.

It was big and black. With two handles. Despite the man's size he had to use two hands to hold it. Nikki knew he would shoot at them. So she faked like she was going to fly to the left and then flew to the right. A perfect fake. The man didn't expect it. Luckily. Because just as Nikki turned to the side, the man fired the gun.

Nikki had expected an ear-splitting *BOOM!* as the cannon-like weapon exploded from close range. However, it was remarkably silent. All she heard was a whizzing sound and then a *poof!* Something tickled the bottom of her leg as she dove away. She looked back to see what had almost hit her. Her eyes detected movement below her.

A thick net was hurtling toward the ground. A net designed to catch someone. Like a power kid, for instance. It was probably the same net that had caught Samantha. The net stopped falling and began moving back up toward the helicopter. It was connected to the big, black gun. He was reeling it back in, like a fisherman pulling in his fishing line. Nikki knew he would try to catch her again. It was time to use her trick—the one she was saving for the right time. Now was definitely the right time.

She reached in her pocket and extracted the gray glove. The man wouldn't be able to shoot at someone he couldn't see. But then she fumbled the glove. She had never dropped one of her powergloves like that before. It skipped off her fingers and dropped like a rock toward the ground, falling much faster than she expected it to.

The man fired the gun again. *Whizzzzzzz!*

Nikki closed her eyes and waited for the spider web of ropes to entangle her.

She heard a faint buzzing sound. A voice yelled from above her. "Flying Chainsaw Chipmunk!" the voice said. It was Spencer. In the heat of the fight against the black STING helicopter, she had forgotten that Spencer still clung to her back.

She didn't feel anything. No ropes. No net. Nothing. Except Spencer on her back.

She opened her eyes slowly. The man was still in the copter doorway. With the gun. But the net wasn't hanging from it anymore. The ropes had been shredded, cut away from the gun. They twirled and twisted as they fell to the earth. *What saved us?* Nikki wondered.

Then she saw it. Something small, arms extended, flaps of skin filled with air, gliding around her. She felt like the thing was defending her. But what was it?

She saw Spencer's hand appear in front of her face. It was cupped slightly, like he was holding something. His hand was empty. "Return to me," Spencer said. Nikki wondered what he meant.

She watched as the flying thing came closer and closer until she could see what it was: A chipmunk, brown with white and black stripes, soared toward her. Its tiny arms were connected to its legs by leathery flaps of skin. The flaps caught the wind and allowed it to fly. Nikki had heard of flying squirrels before, but never flying chipmunks.

The chipmunk was right in front of Nikki now, so close she could have touched it. It swooped in and landed gracefully on Spencer's cupped hand. "Do you like it?" Spencer asked.

"What is it?" Nikki said.

"One of my gadgets. Dexter helped me build it yesterday while you and the power kids were planning the stakeout. I call it Flying Chainsaw Chipmunk."

Nikki stared at the cute little chipmunk. She said, "I understand *Flying* and *Chipmunk*, but what do you mean by *Chainsaw*?"

Spencer chuckled. "Open up, Chippy, and show Aunty Nikki your teeth." The adorable chipmunk grinned and flashed his teeth. Except they weren't really teeth. With a *bzzzzzz!* each "tooth" began to spin rapidly. Each had sharp claws that looked like they could cut through metal. They looked like miniature chainsaws. Suddenly, everything clicked for Nikki. The net had been about to capture them, and then it was shredded, falling to the earth. The little chipmunk's chainsaw teeth had saved them. Spencer had saved them, like he had many times before, with his gadgets.

Nikki was about to thank her friend and tell him what an awesome sidekick he was, when she heard a loud whirring on her right. And then a loud whirring on her left. The sounds were just like the loud whirring sound that the black helicopter was making in front of them.

She glanced to each side, one after the other. Two more black helicopters had arrived. And each had a door open with a masked man with a big gun. A gun with a net. To catch her. She was nearly surrounded. Her only way out was to spin and zoom back. Then she heard it. A fourth whirring sound, from directly behind her. A fourth helicopter. Now she was surrounded.

Even Spencer's Flying Chainsaw Chipmunk wouldn't be able to cut them out of four nets. With a sharp *twang!* the first net was fired. *Twang, twang, twang!* Three more nets were fired.

Nikki knew she would be caught.

3

It's raining Weebles, hallelujah!

Nikki felt the harsh slap of the ropes on her face and her arms and her legs. The ropes quickly surrounded her, and no matter how much she struggled she couldn't seem to find a way out. Spencer's Chainsaw Chipmunk had managed to bite through a few strands of rope but was quickly subdued when a smaller net had hit him, entangling him in tight netting. They had all been captured by STING. Just like Samantha.

Nikki couldn't do anything but watch as the big men on the STING helicopters reeled her and Spencer in. Spencer whispered, "What do we do, El-Grande?" Nikki almost smiled at her friend. She had no idea how he managed to come up with a silly nickname for her when they were in a terrible situation. But she couldn't smile. Things were way too bad for that.

"I have no idea," Nikki whispered back. "I think we just have to hope our friends try to save us, like we tried to save Samantha."

They were really close to the helicopter now. Soon they would be onboard, probably tied up, their arms and legs chained. Prisoners. Nikki felt hopeless.

That's when it happened.

A miracle.

Suddenly the air above her was filled with raucous laughter and giggles, and shrieks and cries of *hoot, hoot!* and *whoop, whoop!* Only one type of creature could make such a funny racket: Weebles!

Dozens of Weebles descended upon Nikki and Spencer, upon the helicopters, gliding down with parachutes. The strange creatures that looked like a cross between a porcupine and a beaver were making all kinds of noises. One of them yelled, "Go Weebletroopers!"

The men on the helicopters jumped back, away from the doors, as the first few Weebles landed. They were kicking and punching and clawing. They looked dangerous. Nikki knew that they weren't really. But the STING guys probably had never seen a Weeble before. They probably didn't even know they existed. Until a few weeks earlier, Nikki hadn't known either, but then she had met one of the funny creatures, and her whole life was changed when he gave her a treasure chest full of powergloves.

A half a dozen Weebles landed on the nets around Nikki and Spencer, too. One was bright green and another was a pinkish hue, while the remaining four were all a standard dull gray color. They began gnawing through the ropes and soon Nikki was free again. She flew high into the air, above the action, and then watched as the helicopters sped away from her, with Weebles clinging to the dark flyers like slugs on wet bark.

"Hip hip hooray!" Spencer shouted.

Nikki reached a hand back over her shoulder and he slapped it. Soon the helicopters faded into the distance, heading back to STING headquarters in Cragglyville. Below her, many of the parachuting Weebles had reached the ground and were running about, frolicking across the vast empty fields. Nikki allowed herself to descend to the earth. Her feet touched down and Spencer clambered from her back. A dark gray Weeble approached them and said, "Hee hee hee, you lost something, Nikki Powergloves?" A gray glove was dangling from his paw.

"My invisibility glove!" Nikki exclaimed. She reached her hand out toward the Weeble, but he ran off, squealing with laughter. "Hey," Nikki said, "that's mine!"

"Hoo hoo hoo! I'm Nikki Powergloves, the greatest child superhero ever!" the Weeble giggled.

Nikki took off after him, once more using her flying power to skim along the field. She was about to catch him, but then he ducked and rolled away from her, changing direction faster than she thought possible. *Weebles are quick little buggers!* Nikki thought. She turned sharply and once more caught up to the spiky little fellow. She stretched her arm out as far as it could go and then lunged at him, grabbing the tips of the gray glove fingers from his furry paw.

"Gotcha!" Nikki exclaimed.

She tumbled across the grass, rolling to a stop a few feet later. The Weeble rolled over to her, doing somersaults across the lush field. "Good game, Nikki," he said.

"Thanks," Nikki said, as she slipped her hand back into the glove. She couldn't stay mad at the funny creature, even if he stole her powerglove. Nikki heard someone talking nearby and wondered if Spencer was chatting with the Weebles. She had barely gotten used to the fact that Weebles could talk just like human beings when they looked just like animals.

But Spencer wasn't talking to the Weebles. He was talking to a group of four kids. The Power Council! They had arrived on the scene and Nikki could tell that Spencer was telling them everything that had happened. He was making big gestures with his hands, first pretending to be a helicopter and then a Weeble. Nikki jogged over to her friends.

She heard a chubby dark-skinned boy say, "We saw the whole thing. Who do you think brought the Weebles?" It was one of the power kids named Freddy Powersocks. He was wearing camouflage-green socks. His body and clothes kept changing color to match the background.

Sometimes he was his normal self and other times he looked just like the grass behind him, like a chameleon. It was one of his powers.

Spencer said, "It was you? Wow, totally-sweet-awesome-cool!"

Nikki said, "Hey, guys. How'd you know we needed help?"

"Hey, Nikki," another boy said. His name was Mike Powerscarves. He was skinny with pasty white skin littered with brown freckles. "Dexter was watching the security cameras on the mountain and saw the helicopter coming a mile away. Then you showed up and it looked like you could use some help."

"Thanks, Dexter," Nikki said to a short, Asian kid standing next to Mike.

From behind a pair of thick glasses that were way too big for his face, Dexter said, "You're welcome." Then he turned to Spencer and said, "Did you use the chipmunk?"

Spencer's face lit up. "Oh yeah! And it worked perfectly, cheep cheep! At least until the other three helicopters arrived."

"That's okay, Spence," Nikki said. "It was a really good try and it's a really cool invention."

A dark-haired girl with deep, dark eyes said, "How did your stakeout go? Did you find out anything about Samantha?" The girl's name was Chilly Weathers. Like Dexter and Spencer, she was a sidekick.

Nikki's face fell. She recounted the story of how they were watching the building and then the helicopters took off and they followed them to the mountain. She concluded by saying, "So we didn't really find out anything. We're no closer to rescuing Samantha than we were before!"

Freddy put a big arm around her shoulder and said, "Don't worry, Nikki. You did the right thing. You might have prevented STING from discovering the Power City. We'll find Samantha. We just need another plan."

Nikki nodded. "I hope so."

Before anyone could say another word, a Weeble ran up and yelled, "Dance party USA!"

4

Who's a better dancer: Nikki or a Weeble named Bo Diddy?

The Weebles surrounded Nikki and the rest of the Power Council. They were all cheering and jumping and dancing around. One of them had a big boom box strapped to his back. Music was blaring from the speakers. The music was fast and upbeat.

Nikki and Spencer looked at each other and laughed. The danger had passed and now it was time to have a little fun. Chilly started doing a funny zombie dance—her arms were extended wildly as she marched in place. Dexter pretended to be a sprinkler while Mike and Freddy moved stiffly, like they were robots.

Soon Nikki and Spencer joined in, dancing alongside the Weebles, celebrating the victory. Nikki shimmied and spun and shook her arms and legs to the beat of the music. Under the heat of the sun she started sweating, but she didn't stop moving. It was so fun!

The Weebles were natural dancers, using every part of their bodies to dance and move. Some were sliding around on their backs, while other spun on their heads, like tops. They did cartwheels and flips and pirouettes.

As Nikki danced, she realized that a circle of Weebles had formed around her. At first she was nervous, but they were cheering for her, so she just kept dancing, going faster and faster. One of the Weebles got pushed into the circle with Nikki, and soon the crowd of Weebles and kids started chanting, "Dance off! Dance off!" Nikki could see that Spencer had a huge grin on his face. He was chanting, too.

The silvery Weeble pranced up to her and said, "Hey, Fly-girl, want to dance against me?"

Nikki shrugged and said, "Bring it on, Fur-ball."

With that, the Weeble started rapping along to the music. He said:

Yo, check it out. Yo, Nikki! Say what?
My name's Bo Diddy and I know how to dance,
I hop and I trot and I flip and I prance,
My moves are like magic, oh you know what I mean,
If you think you can beat me, you must be new to this scene!

While the Weeble rapped, he did a break dance, using his four paws simultaneously to twirl around on the ground. When he finished his song, he stood up on his back paws and raised his front paws above his head. The crowd cheered. A female Weeble with pretty yellow and blue ribbons in her hair yelled, "We love you, Bo Diddy, you're the greatest!!"

Nikki realized that she was against the best dancer amongst all the Weebles. He probably did dance competitions like this one all the time in Weebleville, whereas it was the first time Nikki had ever done anything like it. She didn't know what move to try first. As she was thinking about what to do, she glanced down at her hands. She spotted the blue flying glove and the gray invisibility glove. Her powers! It was her only chance to win!

A moment later she was hovering a few feet above the earth. She made herself invisible and then reappeared. Invisible. And then reappeared. She started doing it over and over again as she began to simultaneously spin and corkscrew in the air. A rhyme came to her. She said:

Hey, Bo Diddy, you be thinkin' you're good,
But I bet your ancestors were chewin' on wood,
If you really had moves you'd know how to fly,
I'm gonna beat you, it's as easy as pie!

Nikki stopped spinning and turning invisible and dropped to the ground, in the dead center of the dance circle. A hush fell over the Weebles. And then one of them yelled, "The Dancing Queen lives!"

The rest of the Weebles went nuts, screaming and whistling and stomping their paws. The Weeble that called himself Bo Diddy approached Nikki. "My Queen," he said, as he kissed Nikki's hand. Like all Weebles, his voice had a heavy New York accent.

Nikki laughed. Out of all her accomplishments since becoming a superhero, she thought she might be most proud of this one. She had out-danced a Weeble!

5

Spencer's big plunger idea

Nikki was back in the Power City with her friends. They were in their favorite room, the one with the two big, soft, purple couches. They were eating pizza, as usual. They all loved pizza, and because one of Mike's powers was to create food from thin air, he regularly "cooked" them a couple of pies.

Everyone was still talking about the dance-off between Nikki and the Weeble. Dexter said, "I've never seen anything so funny in my entire life. Who is this Bo Diddy guy?"

"He was a pretty good dancer," Nikki admitted.

"Yeah, he was ridonkulous!" Spencer agreed.

"I wish Samantha could have seen it," Freddy said glumly.

Nikki was so energized by the dance competition that she had forgotten about the rest of the stuff that had happened. It all came flooding back. The stakeout. The helicopter chase. Nearly being captured by the STING nets. Spencer's Flying Chainsaw Chipmunk. The parachuting Weebles. A lot had happened in a day. And yet Samantha was still captured.

"We need a new plan," Nikki said. "We can't just keep sitting outside the STING building watching them. We have to do something."

"Like what?" Mike asked.

Everyone looked to Nikki. Ever since Samantha had been kidnapped, Nikki had become the unofficial leader of the Power Council. Nikki looked at Spencer and the other sidekicks. Although the power kids were all very talented, it was the sidekicks who came up with a lot of the ideas. They were really smart and creative.

Right on cue, Spencer said, "I have an idea." His lips curled into a big, toothy grin. He almost looked devilish. Nikki knew it was going to be something crazy. Most of Spencer's ideas were crazy. But they also worked. Like the Chainsaw Chipmunk, for example.

"What is it?" Nikki asked.

"Before I get into the details, I want to name my plan. It's called Spencer's Big Plunger Idea, or the Big Plunge for short."

"Sounds interesting," Chilly remarked.

"It is more than interesting," Spencer said. "It's ooka ooka ahkka ahkka, diddly squat stick your head in a coffee pot!"

Nikki and the rest of the kids cracked up laughing. They all loved Spencer's unique way with words. Mike looked at Nikki. "Care to translate?" he asked.

Nikki said, "I wouldn't say I'm perfectly fluent in Spench, as I like to call his funny way with words, but I am pretty good. I would say he was trying to say that his plan is really cool, but in a weird, might-work-might-not kind of way. How'd I do, Spence?"

"Pretty close, Professor-Octopus," Spencer said. Everyone started laughing again. "All I was saying is that my plan is slightly unorthodox. You know, it's something that normal people probably wouldn't try."

"Okay, Spence. Give it to us," Nikki said.

"Okay. The basic concept is that we—and by *we* I mean the sidekicks—design a gimungous plunger to disrupt the flow of water through the pipes in the STING building."

"Gimungous?" Freddy asked.

Spencer explained. "You know, big. Huge, giant, enormous, gigantic, ginormous, hugamungous. In short, a really, really big plunger with incredible sucking power."

"But what will that do?" Nikki asked. "Say you disrupt the water flow—what will that accomplish?"

Spencer's eyes gleamed with excitement. "I have no idea, but it will definitely cause all kinds of problems and will force the STING employees to come out of hiding. Maybe we can recognize a few of them from around Cragglyville. It would be good to know who we're up against."

"I like it," Nikki said. "All those in favor of Spencer's Big Plunger Idea…"

Each kid raised one hand in support. Spencer raised both his hands.

Nikki said, "The plan has been approved by the Council. How soon can you have the gimungous plunger ready?"

Spencer looked at Dexter. Dexter shrugged and said, "We can probably build it in an hour if we all work together."

While Mike delivered the leftover pizza to Weebleville—the city he had built for the Weebles to live in—the other five kids headed to the Lab to work on the plunger. Nikki wasn't sure whether she would be able to help, but wanted to watch.

Sixty three minutes later, Nikki was staring at the biggest plunger she had ever seen. It was truly gimungous, just like Spencer had promised. It had a long, thick, wooden handle that took three of them to lift. At the end of the handle was a massive, bell-shaped, rubber suction cup. It was dull reddish-pink and weighed a ton. Nikki knew she would be the only one strong enough to carry it. But only when she was wearing her super-strength gloves—the purple ones.

Nikki swapped her gray invisibility glove for her purple super-strength one, and kept the blue glove on so she could fly. The power kids left the Power City, heading for Cragglyville by the most direct route possible. They all travelled differently. Nikki flew, of course, carrying the big plunger on her back. The sidekicks sat atop it, all in a row, Spencer and then Dexter and then Chilly. Freddy wore his black and yellow socks and turned into a bumble bee, zipping alongside Nikki. Mike was on the other side with a bright orange scarf. When he wore it, a hovercraft appeared, which he rode surfer-style, rocketing through the air.

Soon they were approaching Cragglyville. The STING building was on the outskirts of town. They landed together, away from the town, in a clearing amidst a dense forest. It was the same forest where Nikki had first met the Weeble. The same forest where she had found the powergloves.

Everyone knew the plan. As soon as they were back on the ground, Freddy changed from a bumblebee back into a boy. He removed his black and yellow socks and replaced them with the brown ones. Each sock had a picture of a shovel on it. They were the same socks he had used to burrow the many tunnels in the Power City, deep within the mountain below Phantom's Peak. They were his digging socks.

The sidekicks hopped onto Mike's hovercraft and he took off into the air. Their job was to watch the building from the outside, to see what would happen when Nikki used the plunger on the building's pipes.

As soon as their friends were gone, Freddy began digging. Nikki had never seen anything like it in her life. Without any tools—no shovels, no picks, no scoops—Freddy scraped and clawed through the dirt like a hound dog searching for a bone. He shoveled the dirt, rocks, and debris with his hands, tossing it between his legs and across the clearing. Nikki had to stand far away from him to avoid being hit by the spray.

Moments later, Freddy had disappeared beneath the surface, as his hole grew wider and deeper. Nikki only had to wait ten minutes for him to come back out. His head popped out of the hole like a gopher's. "We're in business," he said.

He had dug a half-mile tunnel in only ten minutes! Actually, it was even less time, because he had to run back to Nikki, which probably took at least five minutes.

He ducked his head back into the hole and Nikki scrambled after him, dragging the gigantic plunger behind her. She expected to have to get a little bit dirty, crawling on her hands and knees all the way to the STING building, but instead, she was shocked to find that the tunnel was tall enough for her to stand and walk upright in, and plenty big enough to drag the plunger through. Freddy walked beside her. He had a powerful white light strapped to his head, which illuminated the tunnel in front of them.

At first the tunnel was full of roots from the forest above. The natural water pipes dangled from the ceiling of the tunnel, tickling Nikki's hair as she brushed past them. Soon, however, the roots disappeared, and the ceiling and walls became smooth and clean cut. It was as if the tunnel had been dug by a team of professional miners rather than a nine-year-old boy using only his hands.

Abruptly, the tunnel came to an end. There was a thick pipe above them.

"The main water supply for the STING building comes in here," Freddy said.

Nikki nodded and lifted Freddy onto her shoulders. Although he was a big kid, Nikki was easily able to hoist him up because she was wearing her super-strength glove.

Nikki watched her friend work above her. From his pocket, he extracted a flame torch. He worked fast, burning through the metal piping. He said, "Are you prepared to get wet?"

"Whatever it takes," Nikki replied. A trickle of water escaped the crack in the pipe. The trickle became a light spray, which misted onto Nikki face. It felt good. She was hot and sweaty from hiking through the tunnel.

The spray became a burst and then the pipe exploded when Freddy cut completely through it. Gallons of water rushed out and soon Nikki and Freddy were floating next to each other, the water level rising.

"Hurry," Freddy said.

Nikki located the plunger, which was floating nearby. She grabbed it by the wide handle and then looked up. The half of the pipe that led away from the STING building had bent and was dangling from the roof. The important half—the half that led *into* the STING building—was still intact and was dumping water into the tunnel. Nikki wanted to stop the water from raining down on them. She raised the plunger above her head, and with a *pop!* shoved it against the open end of the pipe. Water continued to leak out, past the rubber end of the plunger, but did so at a much slower rate. Nikki pushed hard and heard a satisfying *squish*, as the plunger suctioned to the pipe. The flow of water stopped completely.

"Good job, Nikki!" Mike said encouragingly. "Do you know what to do next?"

"I think so," Nikki said. She had seen her dad use a plunger a couple of times before, when the toilet or sink drain got clogged. He would push the plunger down to get the suction, like Nikki had already done, and then pull it back up to release the suction. He would do it again and again until the water was flowing again. In this case, Nikki wasn't really sure what was going to happen.

She curled the end of her tongue over her upper lip as she concentrated, and then yanked the plunger from the pipe. There was a loud *WHOOSH!* and water began pouring out again. She jammed the plunger back onto the pipe and then ripped it free again. *WHOOSH!* It was like all the water in building pipes was being pulled in different directions. Upwards by anyone using the sinks or toilets and downwards by Nikki and her big plunger. She could hear the water sloshing around in the big pipe.

She started working the plunger faster now. Jamming it on and yanking it off. Jam and yank. Jam and yank. In between each motion, the whooshing and sloshing of the water got more and more powerful, as if it was building up to something. Despite being super-duper strong, Nikki's arms were getting tired. She was worried that she might run out of energy.

She did another plunging motion. And then another. Just when she thought all of her energy had been expended, she did one final plunge and then something happened.

There was no whooshing sound, no slosh of water, not even a trickle of water from the end of the pipe. Instead, the pipe began to groan and rattle. The groaning and rattling got louder and louder until the pipe suddenly moved upwards, jamming itself through the roof of the tunnel and out of sight. The tunnel ceiling crumbled from the force, raining crumbs of dirt and shards of rock down upon Nikki and Freddy. Nikki ducked her head and covered her eyes until she could tell that the small cave-in had ended.

At the same time as she opened her eyes again, she felt her feet touch the ground once more. The tide of water had subsided. It had run down the tunnel, seeking an avenue of escape. Nikki was soaked to the bone, her clothes sopping, her hair wet and messy, and her shoes saturated and squishy. She looked at Freddy.

"What do you think happened?" she asked.

Freddy shrugged. "Something pretty cool, I think. All the water that was coming out of the pipe had to go somewhere. It must have gone up into the STING building!"

Nikki thought about it. Freddy's answer made sense. He was right— the water had to go somewhere. "Okay," she said. "Let's go find the others."

They trudged back through the tunnel, their legs heavy from their damp clothes and wet shoes. They were filthy. The water had muddied the dirt in the tunnel and left a brown sheen on their clothes and skin. It took them twice as long to walk out as it did to walk in.

When they climbed out of Freddy's hole, the rest of the Power Council was already waiting.

Spencer's face was all smiles. He was clearly excited.

"It worked, Miss Plumber!" he said. "It really worked! I wasn't really sure if a plunger could be made to push water in rather than pull water out, but it did, it did!"

Nikki's face lit up. She was glad it worked. But she needed to know what good it had done. "What happened exactly?" she asked.

Spencer yelped, "Spraying water, fountain mayhem, waterfall steps, aquarium offices!"

Mike translated. "What Spencer is saying is that we saw water spraying on some of the windows, probably bathroom windows, and then there was a fountain of water that shot from the roof, high into the air. Water started pouring out the front door, down the building's steps and out into the street. Finally, the offices filled up with water. There were phones and pencils and all kinds of stuff floating around. It was like we were at the aquarium and the office junk was the fish.

"Did all the people get out okay?" Nikki asked.

"I think so," Mike said. They came running out pretty early. Most of them were soaking wet and looked pretty confused. There were about fifty of them and it was pretty crowded. Spencer, did you recognize anyone?"

Spencer was jumping up and down, still excited from the thrill of watching his plan work perfectly. "There were so many of them…"—bounce, bounce—"…that it was hard to see…"—bounce, bounce—"the faces," Spencer said.

"And you didn't see Samantha?" Nikki said.

Spencer, Mike, Dexter, and Chilly all shook their heads.

Nikki frowned. "Then I'm not sure it was much of a success. Seems like we didn't accomplish very much."

Spencer shook his head, like a dog trying to shake water off its fur. "No, no, it *was* a success. We probably stopped the entire STING operation for a couple of days, at least. We can use the time to find Samantha without having to worry about those men in the helicopters."

Nikki hoped her friend was right. She definitely didn't want to see the big men with the net guns again.

Nikki said, "Okay. Good work everyone. We did our best. Now we should all go home and get some sleep. We'll meet in Cragglyville tomorrow and decide what to do."

Everyone agreed and they parted ways. The rest of the Power Council left to go back to the towns they lived in, while Nikki flew Spencer home. Luckily, when Nikki snuck through her front door her mom wasn't home. She wouldn't have been too happy to see her all wet and muddy. And Nikki didn't want to have to answer any hard questions.

She removed her powergloves and wet clothes and then showered and changed. Just as she finished, she heard the front door open. She quickly stuffed her dirty clothes into a bag. She would have to clean and dry them at Spencer's house the following day. She stuffed the bag under her bed for safekeeping.

Exiting her room, she bounded down the stairs, ready to greet her mom. But it wasn't her mom who had come home. It was her dad. And he was *not* happy. Mr. Nickerson was wearing his usual dark suit, dark tie, and black shoes. He was carrying his regular dark work satchel. The only thing different was that he was soaking wet, from head to toe. And he was scowling. Nikki's dad almost never scowled.

It was then that Nikki realized that her dad had been in the STING building.

6

Who is Nikki's dad?

What happened to you, Dad?" Nikki asked.

The scowl was still on his face. He was dripping water all over the carpet. "Plumbing backed up at work," he said. "The whole place flooded."

Nikki had to pretend to be surprised. She raised her eyebrows and opened her eyes wide. "Really?" she said.

Nikki heard the growl of a motor as a blue car pulled into the driveway. Her mom was home. She stepped from the car, closed the door, and walked lightly up the walk to the house. When she saw her husband, she said, "What happened to you?"

He told Nikki's mom what he had just told Nikki. She was genuinely shocked. "I can't believe a little plumbing problem could do all of this"—she waved her hand up and down Mr. Nickerson—"to you."

"Weird, huh?" he said. And then, "I don't think it was just a freak incident. I think someone sabotaged us."

Nikki's heart skipped a beat. She wondered if he had any idea who had done it. But she was afraid to ask. She didn't want to seem overly interested. Luckily, her mom said, "But who could have done such a thing? You don't think it was those vandals again? The ones they call Jimmy Powerboots, Naomi Powerskirts, and Peter Powerhats."

Nikki almost laughed. It sounded weird to hear her mom say the names of her archenemies.

Nikki's dad said, "No, I think it was kids like them, but not them."

Nikki couldn't help but to blurt out, "But what other kids could be like them? They are evil!"

"You're forgetting about the superhero who shares your own name, this Nikki Powergloves character. She and her friends might have done it."

Nikki stopped breathing for a minute. *Her dad suspected Nikki Powergloves! Which meant that STING suspected her, too! But they couldn't possibly know that she was Nikki Powergloves. Her identity was a secret known only to the Power Council.*

She started breathing again, trying to play it cool. "Really, Dad? I wouldn't think Nikki Powergloves would do that, she's one of the good guys, right?"

"I agree with Nikki, dear," Mrs. Nickerson said. "I wouldn't be throwing around wild accusations. Nikki Powergloves has done a lot of good for this town."

"I know she has," Mr. Nickerson said, "but she also has a lot of power, which makes her dangerous, just like the bad kids. If she ever decides to use her powers for evil, she could hurt a lot of people."

Nikki suddenly felt hot and angry. All she had done since becoming a superhero was help people. Well, there was that one accident where she created a massive storm and destroyed a bunch of the farmers' crops and fences and stuff, but she had made up for it by using her powers to fix everything. Ever since, she—with the help of Spencer and the Power Council—had fought against Jimmy and the Power Outlaws to protect Cragglyville. How dare her dad accuse her of being bad? It was the STING helicopters that attacked her, not the other way around. She was just defending herself.

Nikki knew she needed to calm down, so she said, "I'm going to hang out in my room until dinner," and then climbed the stairs to the second floor.

"Okay, honey," Nikki's mom said. "Dinner will be ready in a half hour."

Once inside her room, she closed the door gently. As usual, Mr. Miyagi was sleeping on the rug on her bedroom floor. Mr. Miyagi was Nikki's gray Scottish terrier. He was the best dog in the world. He was friendly, smart, and very protective of Nikki. But he also liked taking naps. He liked her rug because it was almost always warm from the sunlight that came through Nikki's window.

Nikki rubbed him behind the ears and he stirred sleepily. His eyes blinked open and he licked his lips. "Have a good nap, buddy?" Nikki asked.

Mr. Miyagi licked Nikki's hand as if to say, "All naps are good, Nikki."

"I thought so," Nikki said. Another reason Nikki loved Mr. Miyagi so much was because he was a good listener. And she really needed to talk to someone. "Hmmm," Nikki said. "It would be better if I could understand what you were saying to me." Nikki knew there was a way she could have a conversation with Mr. Miyagi but she had never used it before. She hadn't tried it before because she was afraid of scaring him. But she was desperate now. She had no other choice.

Nikki reached in her pocket and plucked out a tiny box. She placed it in the center of the floor, away from the bed and where her dog was lying. A string was attached to the box's lid. She pulled the string sharply and the lid popped off. Immediately the box began to grow, bubbling and bouncing until it was the size of a real treasure chest, taking up almost half of the open space in her room.

She reached into the magical chest and rummaged through the powergloves that were stored inside. She was looking for the brown ones with the paw prints on them. She located them and tugged them onto each hand. She replaced the lid on the powerchest and watched as it shrunk again. Then she said, "Don't get scared and start barking, Mr. Miyagi, okay?"

Her dog chuffed as if to say, "What do you think I am, a 'fraidy cat?"

Nikki closed her eyes and imagined what it would be like to be a small dog, one that looked similar to Mr. Miyagi, except brown. Even though she hadn't moved a muscle, she felt the soft carpet underneath her hands. Except she knew something was different about her hands. They weren't hands—not anymore. She opened her eyes and looked down to see her paws planted firmly on the carpet. She had transformed into a dog!

Mr. Miyagi was looking at her curiously, his head cocked to the side. He looked so cute and funny that Nikki couldn't help but to giggle. It came out as a high-pitched bark. *Arf, arf!* she said. But in her mind it sounded just like her normal girlish laughter.

Mr. Miyagi said, "You're a dog, Nikki." Nikki knew he was barking softly, but to her it sounded just like English. She could understand every word that he barked out.

"Sorry, Mr. Miyagi, I should have done this sooner," Nikki barked.

Mr. Miyagi looked down at Nikki's front paws. Nikki followed his gaze and saw that her paws were hidden inside brown rubber gloves. She knew they were the same gloves she was wearing just a minute earlier, but they had molded to her dog paws. As usual, they were still a perfect fit for her.

"Let me guess, those gloves turned you into a dog?" Mr. Miyagi asked.

"Yes."

"It's nice to finally talk to you for real," Mr. Miyagi said.

"You, too," Nikki replied. "Say, I've always wanted to ask you, why do you like to be rubbed on your tummy so much?"

Mr. Miyagi laughed. It came out as a hoarse squeal. "Good question. I don't even know the answer. I just love it! It just feels wonderful!"

Nikki laughed. "I will try to rub your tummy at least one time every day then."

"Nikki?" Mr. Miyagi said.

"Yeah?"

"What's bothering you?"

Nikki was amazed at how smart her dog really was. He could sense that she wasn't herself. Not because she was a dog, but because he knew her that well. He was more than just her dog. He was her friend. Just like Spencer, or Mike, or Freddy, or Samantha.

Nikki said, "I don't even know who my dad really is."

Mr. Miyagi nodded his head up and down. "I'm surprised it took you this long to notice," he barked.

"What do you mean?" Nikki asked her wise dog.

"Try to remember the signs."

Nikki closed her doggie eyes and tried to concentrate. She started moving backwards through time until she was four-years-old. It was the farthest thing back that she could remember. It was her birthday. Her mom was asking her how old she was. She saw herself lifting her hand and showing four fingers to her mom. *This many*, she had said. *You're right!* her mom had exclaimed.

Then she saw her dad. He was there, too. He was carrying a cake with four candles. He placed it in front of Nikki. She was so happy.

But then his phone rang. He looked at it and said, *I'm sorry, Nikki. There's an emergency at work, I have to go.* He shrugged and then left. At the time Nikki was confused. What could be more important than her birthday?

As she got older she learned that sometimes grownups have important things to do. She always assumed that her dad had important things to do. But whenever she asked him about those things, he could never really explain them to her.

Her memory flashed forward two years.

She was six-years-old now. She was playing in the backyard with Mr. Miyagi. She was throwing a Frisbee and watching him chase it. Her dad had come out to watch. *Throw it far, Daddy!* she had said to him. Her dad smiled and took the Frisbee and then slung it across the entire backyard, farther than Nikki had even thought was possible. Mr. Miyagi ran after it happily, wagging his tail. Nikki said, *I wish I had super powers so I could throw as far as you, Daddy.* Her dad surprised her by saying, *No one should be more powerful than someone else, Nikki. Always remember that.* She always wondered why he had said that.

She fast-forwarded three more years, to just a few days earlier. Cragglyville was under attack. By the Power Outlaws. Naomi and Jimmy and Peter. They were doing bad things. Smashing windows, toppling trees, bashing buildings. Peter Powerhats was trapping people's feet in stone. Her dad was there. He had been trapped in stone, too.

Nikki and her friends had arrived on the scene. They were there to fight the Power Outlaws. There to save Cragglyville. There to save her dad. Nikki was wearing her costume to protect her secret identity. Her long braid was wrapped around the front of her face, covering her eyes. She could see out through the eye holes that Spencer had made for her.

She had saved her dad that day, but she distinctly remembered the way he had looked at her. He didn't seem happy like he should have been. He had just been rescued and yet…he seemed like he was angry. His eyebrows were tightly formed into a V and his lips were in a straight line. He had said thanks to her, but he didn't really seem thankful. Not really.

The memory vanished and Nikki opened her eyes. Mr. Miyagi was still looking at her. "Do you see what I mean?" he barked.

"Yes," Nikki replied. "I should have known there was something odd about where he worked. He works for STING, doesn't he?. He's one of the people trying to catch me and my friends! What do I do, Mr. Miyagi?"

Mr. Miyagi scratched behind his ear thoughtfully. "You need to find a way to convince him that it's wrong to kidnap the power kids. That not all of them are bad like the Power Outlaws."

Nikki nodded. "Thanks, Mr. Miyagi. I will try my best."

She was about to change back into a girl when she remembered something else that she wanted to ask her dog. "Oh, I almost forgot. I've always wanted to ask you whether you liked the name I gave you: Mr. Miyagi?"

Mr. Miyagi grinned a doggie-grin at her. "I love it!" he barked. He might have barked a little too loudly, because just then the door burst open. Nikki had forgotten to lock the door!

Her dad started to say, "Are you okay, Nikki, I heard Mr. Miyagi bark—" but then he stopped. He was staring at Nikki the dog. "Where did you come from?" he said.

Nikki knew she was in big trouble. She had only one choice.

She ran!

Mr. Nickerson tried to grab her, but she managed to squeeze between his legs and out the door. She heard his footsteps right behind her as she scampered down the stairs. She cut across the family room and into the kitchen. Her claws scraped across the tile floor and her mom exclaimed, "Oh my gosh!" Seconds later she was through the doggie door at the base of the back door. She spilled into the backyard, panting heavily. But she didn't have time to catch her breath before she heard the door open behind her. She raced around the corner of the house, out of sight from the back door or windows. Immediately she changed back into human form and pulled her brown gloves off, hurriedly stuffing them into her pockets.

After taking two deep breaths, Nikki walked around the corner of the house and back into the yard. Mr. Nickerson was standing in the grass, scanning the yard, his hands on his hips and his face formed into a frown.

"Hi, Dad," Nikki said. "Did you see that dog, too?"

His head jerked around and he looked at her. He seemed startled by her sudden appearance. "Oh, hi, Nikks. Where'd you come from?" he said.

"I had just come through the side gate when a little brown dog ran past me and squirmed through that hole in the fence. I swear she looked like she could have been Mr. Miyagi's sister!"

Mr. Nickerson frowned again. "How did you know the dog was a girl?" he asked.

Nikki wasn't expecting the question. She tried to answer, but all that came out was, "Uh, oh, um, well…"

Her dad stood there waiting, looking at her strangely, his frown getting deeper. His face looked all wrinkly. She had never seen it that way.

Finally, she found her voice: "I dunno, Dad, it just looked like a girl to me. Could've been a boy, I suppose." She knew her answer was lame, but it was all she could think of.

"It came from inside the house," her dad said.

"What did?" Nikki said.

"The dog."

"Oh."

"From your room."

"My room? How did it get in there?"

"I was going to ask you the same thing."

"I dunno. I was out here playing in the yard."

"I thought you were just coming from the front to the back—through the gate."

Nikki was getting flustered. She felt hot. Her face felt like it was turning red. She felt sweat on her forehead. Her knees were shaking a little. Her dad kept catching her in her little white lies. If she said the wrong thing he might suspect she was Nikki Powergloves. And then he might call his big, strong buddies with the masks and the black helicopters. And then they would come to take her away to some prison where they would lock her up and throw away the key and feed her stale bread and water. She didn't want to go to prison!

"Uh, yeah. I meant I was just playing outside. First I was in the front, and then I decided to come to the back. Anyway, I have no idea

39

how the dog got in my room, maybe Mr. Miyagi invited the dog in to play. I think he should be allowed to have friends, too, don't you think?"

At first her dad continued to scowl at her, but then suddenly his face changed, as if he had just swallowed a happy pill. His normal smile was back and his eyes sparkled with affection. He looked like he loved her again. She was beginning to worry, but maybe there was still hope.

Like Mr. Miyagi had said, she needed to convince him that Nikki Powergloves and her friends were good and should just be left alone.

7

The Power Trappers!

The next day Nikki followed her dad to work. He wasn't going to the STING building. Because it was flooded. Because Nikki had flooded it. He had told her mom that his government agency set up a temporary office in another building in downtown Cragglyville. Except he didn't go into Cragglyville. Nikki knew he didn't, because she was flying high above his car as he drove along. She didn't have time to tell the rest of the Power Council what she was doing, so she was all alone. She didn't even have time to tell Spencer.

When her dad reached the intersection that led to Cragglyville, he turned the other way, away from town. Which meant that he had lied to her mom. Which scared Nikki.

He continued on down a long stretch of road that meandered past acres and acres of farmland, and then turned onto a road that Nikki had never been down before. The road entered a wooded area, with tall trees on each side. She watched as her dad slowed his car and then made a sharp turn directly into the woods. He was going to crash into the trees!

But he didn't crash. In fact, she could still make out the movement of his dark car between the crisscrossing tree branches that formed a canopy over the forest. Evidently, there was a hidden road or trail, wide enough for him to drive his car down.

She continued to follow him until the secret road led to a large clearing in the woods. A lone cabin stood in the center of the clearing. It was made out of big, thick logs that had been cut and skinned of all bark, and then painted deep brown. A rustic stone chimney rose on one side of the cabin. A wisp of smoke rose from the chimney. A dozen cars were haphazardly parked around the cabin. They were all dark colors, like black or navy blue. Nikki's dad parked next to a big, black truck.

He got out and went to the cabin. Nikki descended, trying get a better view. She was careful to stay behind him, out of his field of vision. She watched as he knocked on the door. She counted the number of knocks. *One, two, three…eight, nine, ten.* She didn't know why she counted, but felt like she should. It was something Spencer would do. He always said to pay attention to the details, because they could be important.

On the tenth knock, the door opened. A man let Nikki's dad through the door. Nikki knew right away he was one of the goons from the helicopters. Her heart sank. Until this point, she had hoped that maybe her dad worked for STING, but didn't really know what they were doing—didn't know that they were capturing power kids. But he knew everything. He might have even been in the helicopters when they attacked Nikki, or when they captured Samantha.

She had to stop them. She had to stop her dad. But first she had to get closer.

Nikki flew away from the clearing and into the woods. She quickly swapped one of her flying gloves for a gray invisibility glove. Once she was invisible, she went back to the cabin. She walked right up to it boldly, because she knew no one could see her. The first window she checked out was covered by drapes—she couldn't see anything. She

42

could hear voices, but they sounded dull and far away through the glass. The second window was the same, no good. When she got to the third window, she saw that not only was it uncovered, but it was also open a crack to let fresh air into the cabin. *Perfect!* she thought.

While peeking through the dirty glass, she listened to the conversation inside.

There were four big, strong guys in the room, sitting around a rectangular, wooden table. They had glasses filled with an amber liquid. At the head of the table was her dad. He looked small compared to the bodybuilders around him. Her dad was speaking. Not speaking, more like yelling. He was angry again.

"You're incompetent!" he yelled. "All of you! Not only did you not capture Nikki Powergloves when she was right in front of you, but then you let her flood our headquarters. How is that possible?"

The big guys looked uncomfortable. They all had their heads down, like they were embarrassed. They were fidgeting, tapping their toes, scratching their heads. The whole scene seemed opposite to how you would expect a room full of big, strong guys to look. Nikki thought they should look confident. But they looked weak, pathetic. Her dad was clearly their boss.

The biggest of the big guys said, "I know we had her, but then these crazy creatures started falling from the sky. There must have been hundreds of them; there was nothing we could do!"

Mr. Nickerson's face got even redder. There was a vein on his forehead that was bulging out. It looked like it was about to pop. "Nothing you could do!?" he roared. "You're supposed to be Power Trappers!" He slammed his fist down on the table. The glasses of liquid shuddered and one toppled over, spilling onto the floor.

But Nikki barely even noticed the spill. She was too busy thinking about what her dad had just said. *Power Trappers!* That's what the men in the helicopters were called. It made sense. They had guns that shot nets, rather than bullets or lasers. Trap guns. To trap kids with powers. They were Power Trappers. Literally. And Nikki and her friends were apparently next on their list. Nikki wondered how many other power kids they had captured. *But why?* she wondered.

Her dad answered her unspoken question without even knowing it. He said, "Look, guys, these so-called power kids can't be out roaming the streets, flaunting their powers and fighting each other. The government has to get control of the situation. Once we have all the power kids rounded up, our scientists will be able to concentrate on seeing if we can take their powers from them. Powers like the ones they have are extremely valuable. They could be worth millions, no, *billions* of dollars."

"We understand that," the biggest guy said.

"Do you?" Nikki's dad said, throwing his hands over his head. "Do you really? Because I don't think you're trying hard enough."

"But we've captured three of them already." *Three!* Nikki thought. Samantha and two others. She wondered who the other two kids were—whether they were good or evil.

"Three is nothing," Mr. Nickerson said. "We hired you, trained you, and paid you to catch all twelve kids."

Nikki almost yelled out, "Twelve kids!" but managed to slap a hand over her mouth and control herself. Although they wouldn't be able to see her, they most definitely would be able to hear her through the open window, just like she was able to hear them. They would know someone had been eavesdropping.

Nikki's mind was racing. *Twelve kids!* She counted them in her head. She was one. The Power Council—Samantha who was captured, Mike, and Freddy—were numbers two, three, and four. The Power Outlaws—Jimmy, Naomi, and Peter—were five, six, and seven. According to what she had just heard, there were two other power kids who had been captured, they made eight and nine. That meant there were three other power kids out there! She didn't know how her dad knew all this stuff, but she believed him. He seemed to know a lot of things.

She needed to tell the others. They would need to know if they were going to defeat the Power Trappers.

8

Nikki's second power games

They were sitting on the purple couches, in the room that had all the pictures of the power kids on the walls. They were getting bored of pizza, so Mike whipped up hamburgers and French fries. Nikki knew her mom wouldn't be too happy if she knew her daughter was eating so much junk food. Nikki would recommend that Mike create salads and fruit for the next meal.

Between mouthfuls, Nikki told the Power Council what she had found out while at the STING cabin in the woods. Spencer was the first to comment.

"Holy nickerbockers!" he exclaimed.

"I almost shouted the same thing when I heard it, too," Nikki joked.

Freddy said, "How does your dad know all this stuff?"

"I dunno," Nikki said. "Through work, I guess. I think STING is pretty powerful."

Mike said, "We have to fight back. We can't let these Power Trappers catch us. And we still have to find and rescue Samantha."

"I know," Nikki said. "I know we can do it, but we have to get better at using our powers. We have to practice."

"Does that mean we're going to have another power games?" Freddy asked.

"Yes," Nikki said.

Spencer clapped his hands excitedly. "That's a great idea, Banana-Split! I'll go tell the Weebles."

Nikki grinned. She was excited, too. She had only been in one power games so far, but she had loved it. And she had won! She was ready to challenge herself again, to see if she could take on the best powers of her friends. Only then would she be ready to face the Power Trappers…and her dad.

While Spencer and the other sidekicks ran off to Weebleville to tell the Weebles about the power games, Nikki, Freddy, and Mike made their way to the training center. It was where the power games would be held. Just like before, the power games would be a chance for the power kids to practice with their powers, without the help of their sidekicks. The last power kid standing at the end would be declared the winner.

To get to the training room, they had to walk down a few tunnels. Each had a different theme. The first tunnel was filled with sand, which made it hard to walk. Protruding from the walls were palm trees and big umbrellas. It was called the beach tunnel.

The next tunnel was completely made of candy and chocolate. There were lollipops poking from the ceiling and walls. Candy bars were stacked like bricks on every side. Chewing gum periodically fell from gaps in the roof. The walls were solid chocolate. After Mike had built it, he called it his *Ode to Willy Wonka and the Chocolate Factory*, which was one of his favorite movies. They called it the Wonka tunnel for short. As they passed through the tunnel, Nikki grabbed a lollipop and two candy bars from the walls. She wanted to make sure she had plenty of energy for the power games.

They turned down the next tunnel, which was built completely from Lego blocks. While they walked, Nikki munched on the two candy bars and then sucked on the lollipop. When they reached the door to the training room, Nikki finished off the rest of the lollipop with a big *crunch!* It was time to play.

Nikki opened the tiny door to the room and shimmied through on her belly. The crowd roared.

Although it had only taken them a few minutes to get from the purple couch room to the training center, somehow the bleachers were already full. Spencer and the sidekicks were sitting amongst a throng of Weebles, cheering and whistling. As loud as Spencer was, the Weebles were even louder. They yelled all kinds of stuff, like, "Power kids, power kids, you are silly power kids!" and, "Ratatatat, the power kids are back!" One even yelled, "Nikki, Nikki, Nikki, hey! Nikki, Nikki, Nikki, yay!" Nikki felt like a celebrity.

When they were all inside, Nikki looked at Mike and Freddy. She wasn't sure who would start the competition. Normally it was Samantha who started it. Mike said, "You do it, Nikki."

Nikki shivered with excitement. She mustered all the energy that she could, and yelled, "Let the power games begin!" The crowd cheered loudly. She could hear Spencer yelling, "Hoot hoot!" in a high-pitched voice.

Nikki reached in her pocket and extracted her powerchest. She quickly opened it and searched for the right powergloves to use. She remembered back to the last power games. She had won by changing into a lion using her brown gloves. Mike and Freddy would be expecting her to try the same thing, so she would need to use a different tactic to surprise them.

Just before choosing her gloves, Nikki glanced up at the bleachers. Spencer had started "the wave" and all the Weeble and sidekicks were standing up and raising their arms above their heads each time the wave passed by them. Nikki laughed. Only Spencer would think to do something like that.

She made up her mind and plucked a red glove and a peach glove from the chest. The red glove had a picture of a flame on it, while the

48

peach one had two identical stick figures etched into the rubbery surface.

After pulling on the gloves, Nikki scanned the training room, looking for her opponents. The room was huge, as big as a football stadium. It was filled with all kinds of cool stuff, like tackling dummies, climbing ropes, and metal robots. Mike and Freddy were nowhere to be found.

The first thing Nikki did was use the power of the peach glove. She had only used it twice before. Once to try it out on Spencer, and once to save the Cragglyville Bank from getting blown up by a bomb planted by Jimmy Powerboots. She couldn't wait to try it a third time.

She thought hard about what it would be like to look just like Samantha. It was a dirty trick, but there were no real rules in the power games, except that no sidekicks were allowed to help the superheroes.

Suddenly, Nikki felt a little bit taller and her legs seemed heavier. Like they had grown. She saw her reflection in one of the metal robots. The image was crinkled and distorted but she was still able to see well enough to know: She looked exactly like Samantha Powerbelts. She even had a bright orange belt on. Nikki smiled. Freddy and Mike were in for the shock of their lives.

Nikki crept along the base of one of the climbing walls, listening for signs of the other two power kids. She didn't hear anything. Didn't see anything. They were hiding.

Just as she rounded the corner of the climbing wall, Nikki's cheek was stung by something flat and hard. Her head twisted and her eyes began to well up with tears. "Ouch!" she exclaimed, raising a hand to her face. Her cheek felt hot. She looked all around her to see what had hit her, but couldn't see anything. *Smack!* Her other cheek was slapped, forcing her head to twist the other way. Now both her cheeks were hot and stinging. Who was attacking her? And where was it coming from?

Then she remembered.

One night, not that long ago, Spencer had broken one of the three rules of Weebleville: Never feed the Weebles after midnight. Of course,

Spencer just *had* to find out what would happen, so he fed a Weeble. The Weeble grew into a giant Godzilla-Weeble and rampaged through Weebleville. Until Freddy and Samantha had stopped it. Freddy had helped by using one of his powers. It was called distance slap. And Nikki knew it's what he was doing to her now. He could slap her from really far away, without ever even touching her. It was a great power. But not so great now that it was being used against her. Nikki could only think of one way to stop him.

She stepped out into the open. "Wait, Freddy," she said. Even Nikki was amazed how her voice sounded just like Samantha's. "It's me. Samantha. I escaped."

"Oh my gosh," she heard Freddy say. She tilted her ears to track his voice. Soon she spotted him, high above her on a swinging platform attached to the roof.

"Wow, how'd you get up there?" Nikki asked, still pretending to be Samantha.

From below, Nikki could see his socks. From memory she knew that the peach-colored sock that matched her peach glove gave Freddy the distance-slap power. His other sock was gray. Nikki had no idea what power that one gave him.

Instead of answering her question, Freddy said, "How'd you escape, Samantha?"

Nikki said, "It's hard to hear you. Come down here and I'll tell you all about it."

Freddy shrugged and leapt off the platform. Nikki gasped. He was going to kill himself! He was about fifty feet up—there was no way he could survive a jump from that height.

But Freddy didn't splat on the ground like Nikki was expecting. He didn't even fall. Not really. He really just sort of glided down. She didn't see any wings or parachute or cape or anything that might explain how he was able to do it. And yet he did it.

When he landed next to her, Nikki said, "Cool power, Freddy."

Freddy looked at her strangely. "C'mon, Samantha, you've seen me do it a million times before. It's just my anti-gravity sock." Nikki froze. She knew she had made a mistake. Freddy said, "Hey, wait a minute, you're not Samantha, are you?"

Nikki reacted quickly. Flames danced through her mind. And then the same flames were dancing around Freddy. Using the power of her red glove, she had created a circle of fire around her friend. "Ooh, ah, ooh, ah, that's hot!" Freddy yelped.

"Say uncle," Nikki said.

"Uncle, uncle," Freddy said. "Just turn off the flames, please!"

The flames died away. They didn't so much as leave a ring of black on the floor. It was as if they were never there. They were magic flames, after all.

"Good one, Nikki," Freddy said. "I really thought you were Samantha for a minute."

Nikki smiled and turned back into herself. She could hear the Weebles tittering like excited monkeys in the stands. Spencer yelled something. It sounded like, "Wikki Nikki, walkie talkie, metal kettle, rip roar, hob nob, goooooo Nikki!" She could never be sure *what* Spencer was saying, but she knew for sure that he was cheering her on. And that counted for something.

Now if she could just find Mike. As she scanned the room she wondered what color scarf he would be wearing. She had seen a few of them before. She knew the green one allowed him to create food from thin air. She had seen him do it a bunch of times. But he wouldn't be wearing that one. Maybe he would be wearing the brown striped scarf, like he had at the last power games. It made him spin like a tornado. Or he could be wearing the red and yellow polka dotted one, like he had when Nikki and the Power Council fought against Naomi and the Power Outlaws. That scarf had made Mike break up into ten smaller Mike's, as if there was an army of Mike's! She hoped he wouldn't use that one. It would be hard enough to defeat one Mike, let alone ten.

After she had been sneaking around for about ten minutes unable to find Mike, the crowd was growing restless. The Weebles were starting to boo. They wanted action, but it wasn't Nikki's fault that Mike was hiding from her. But then—

Finally she found him.

Or he found her, rather.

While she was creeping along the side of a big stone wall, she heard a rumble from above her. She looked up to see three large barrels tumbling toward her. She felt like the crocodiles must feel in *Donkey Kong Country* when Donkey Kong throws barrels at them. She pushed off hard with her right foot, took a big step with her left foot, and then dove as far as she could.

She was lucky. Luckier than the crocodiles usually were in *Donkey Kong*.

The barrels crashed to the floor, splintering into a thousand pieces. It would have hurt. She would have lost the power games if she had been hit. They missed though—just barely. Lying on her back, Nikki looked up, at the top of the stone wall. There stood Mike, his hands on his hips, grinning widely. Something was different about him. Something *BIG!*

Coming out of his butt was a massive green tail! It was scaly and had three long spikes at the end. It looked like a dinosaur tail. He was wearing a white scarf with green and red polka dots on it. It was a very festive scarf. And apparently it allowed him to grow the dinosaur tail, which he had then used to slap the barrels off the wall.

Nikki needed a minute to collect her thoughts, so she scrambled to her feet and ran away. She heard a *thud!* behind her and looked back to see Mike on the ground. He had leapt from the wall. His tail had probably helped to cushion the fall. He started to chase her, his spiky tail swinging wildly behind him.

Nikki ran as fast as she could run, and suddenly she was wishing she had her orange gloves on, the ones that gave her super-speed. She passed a giant red bowling ball and ducked behind it, trying to catch her breath.

She changed. She was no longer Nikki. Well, at least she no longer looked like Nikki Powergloves. Instead, she looked like Freddy Powersocks. Her skin was dark. She could see her belly protruding out past her feet.

Mike burst around the big bowling ball. He almost ran right into Nikki. "Freddy!" he yelled. "Which way did she go?"

"I dunno," Nikki said in Freddy's voice. Mike's guard was down. He really believed he was talking to Freddy. Nikki took advantage of the opportunity. "Or maybe she's right here!" she yelled, simultaneously turning back into Nikki and creating a ball of fire. The fireball exploded from her fingertips and collided with Mike's tail, which turned black and fell off. Mike tripped over the charred remains of his dinosaur tail and fell onto his back. His eyes were wide with fear.

Nikki pointed a finger at him. "Say it," she ordered.

"Uncle," he said.

And then there were Weebles all around her, singing, "Olayyyyy, olay olay olay!" and, "Weeee are the championsss, my frie-end!" She had done it again. Nikki had won two power games in a row!

Her smile was a mile wide, until a smallish Weeble with scruffy fur and a strange patch of blue bristles amidst his mostly-gray coloring approached her. Like the other Weebles, he had a strong New York accent. He said, "Nice job, Nikki. I bet you'll move up at least two spots in the rankings! You might even be number one!"

She had no idea what he was talking about.

9

The funky chicken

Bang—bam—BOOM! The sky had been thundering for over an hour. The crashes and smashes of the storm echoed throughout the Power City. Although Nikki couldn't see outside, she knew that a summer storm that sounded this loud usually included bright flashes of lightning and torrential downpours. She was glad she was inside. And dry.

The thrill of winning her second power games in a row had worn off, and Nikki and the rest of the Power Council were back in the purple couch room waiting for the storm to pass. The others were talking. Nikki was thinking about her dad.

She missed him. Not the man with the frown who commanded the attention of a bunch of big men in a remote cabin, but the quick-to-smile man who she looked up to, the man who gave her piggyback rides and bought her juicy hot dogs at the baseball game. She was scared of the man in the cabin. Because he wasn't her dad. Not the dad that she knew. She needed to talk to him, to tell him how she felt.

Crash! Another peal of thunder shook the mountain. Nikki yawned. Suddenly she was very tired. It was crazy how fast time moved when they were in the Power City. She still hadn't gotten used to it. She could sleep for four or five nights in the mountain and only a day would pass in Cragglyville. Because she was spending so much time in the Power City, it was as if she was making the summer holidays last even longer.

"Earth to Nikkiiii," Spencer said.

"Huh?" Nikki said.

"I've called your name five times, Doodle-Bug," Spencer said. Nikki looked around. All the kids were staring at her.

"Oh," she said. "I must have spaced out. I was just thinking…"

"About your dad?"

Nikki made eye contact with Spencer. He always seemed able to read her mind. "Yeah," she admitted.

"I know," Spencer said, "I'm shocked by the whole thing, too. I never would have thought your dad would—"

"Be one of the bad guys?" Nikki interrupted.

"I wasn't going to say that," Spencer said. "I was going to say 'be involved in something like this.' He might not really be bad, Nikki. He is just taking orders from someone higher up who thinks that kids having powers is a bad thing."

"I don't know…" Nikki mused. "It sounded like he agreed that the power kids are dangerous."

Mike said, "Well, we kind of *are* dangerous, Nikki. At least we could be, if we wanted to be. Like Naomi and Jimmy. Peter, too. They could all do a lot of damage. They already have done a lot of bad things, and they would have done more if we hadn't stopped them."

"Then why doesn't my dad go after them? Why did he have to kidnap Samantha? She helped stop the Power Outlaws, remember? Just like we all did."

Mike nodded. "I know, Nikki. It doesn't make sense. But the STING people might just be scared, because they don't understand everything. I mean, we don't even understand everything. Like where did the powerchests come from? And why were they given to us? And where the heck did the Weebles come from? I mean seriously, they're crazy!"

Spencer laughed. "I have to agree with Mike there. The Weebles are one hundred percent certifiably insane, and that's sayin' a lot, coming from me."

Everyone laughed, even Nikki. Not for the first time, or the last time, she was glad Spencer was her best friend, and that he was her sidekick. She yawned again. "I think I might get some sleep," she said.

Everyone agreed to go to bed, so they made their way to the bunk room without even eating dinner, which was normal for life in the Power City. They usually only ate breakfast and lunch while they were inside the mountain.

As soon as Nikki's head hit her bottom-bunk pillow, she drifted asleep. Spencer wasn't even halfway up the ladder to the top bunk yet.

She awoke when she heard a noise. Her eyes flickered open, and she saw Spencer crouched next to her bed. "You've got to see this, Chimichanga," he said.

"See what?" Nikki asked. She rubbed her face to get the sleep out of her eyes.

"The funky chicken."

Nikki heard her friend's words, but had no idea what they meant. Normally, Spencer spoke an entire language that was all his own, one that only he could understand. Sometimes Nikki could grasp the meaning, and other times she couldn't. This time she couldn't.

"Spencer, can you please speak English?" Nikki said.

Spencer grinned. "Actually, I am," he said, which made Nikki even more confused. He had said, "the funky chicken," which made absolutely no sense to Nikki. "Just follow me, okay, Beanie-Baby?"

Nikki wanted to ask him more questions about what the heck a *funky chicken* was, and why it was so important, but she managed to climb out of bed without saying another word. She was already fully dressed, because the power kids always slept in whatever clothes they were wearing when they left home.

Spencer led Nikki down a couple of tunnels and straight to the room with the purple couches. The rest of the Power Council was already there, watching TV. Catchy dance music came from the speakers. Mike and Freddy were pointing and laughing at whatever was on the screen. Dexter had hopped up on the table and was dancing around. Chilly was nodding her head to the beat.

"What's going on?" Nikki asked as she approached.

Without speaking, Mike handed her a warm plate full of waffles and syrup, and then pointed at the screen. Nikki's stomach growled when she smelled the delicious aroma. She cut a bite of waffle, mixed it around in the syrup, and stuffed it in her mouth before looking at the TV.

She almost choked on the food.

Not because the food was bad.

Because of what she saw on the TV.

A chicken.

No, a *funky* chicken. Before seeing what she had just seen on the screen, she had no clue what a funky chicken was. But now she knew. She was looking at one.

The picture was coming from downtown Cragglyville. Of course. It seemed to be where all of Nikki's adventures occurred. She had no idea why Cragglyville was such a hotspot for weird things. It seemed to her that things like what had been happening in Cragglyville would be more suited to Las Vegas, or San Francisco. Not Cragglyville. Cragglyville was just a small farm town.

There was a big chicken on the screen. Bigger than normal chickens. It was about Nikki's size, brown in color, with big dark eyes and ruffled feathers. It was possible that someone was wearing a costume, trying to be funny or convince people to go to Kentucky Fried Chicken or something, but somehow Nikki knew it was a real chicken. And boy was it funky!

Loud music was coming from somewhere and it was dancing up a storm, spinning and kicking and moving its wings all over the place. Sometimes it flopped on the ground like a worm, and other times it spun on its butt. Once it even spun on its head! That chicken was an amazing dancer. It was even better than Nikki had been when she defeated Bo Diddy in the dance competition.

The camera panned over to a sign that had been nailed to a tree, near where the funky chicken was getting all funky. The sign said, "Funky Chick'n."

"Told you," Spencer said. He was grinning.

"How do you think it got there?" Nikki asked.

Spencer said, "I dunno, but a lot of weird things keep happening. It's been almost a week since we defeated the Power Outlaws. I bet Naomi and Jimmy are behind it."

"Oh no, Spence! Do you really think so? What could they possibly use a funky chicken for?"

"Attract attention, for one thing. The people of Cragglyville will come to see the funny, dancing chicken. You know, to take pictures and laugh and stuff. It only started dancing a few minutes ago and already it's all over the news. People are going to start arriving soon. And then the Power Outlaws will strike! Run for your lives!"

"We have to go back, right now!" Nikki said. She slid her mostly uneaten plate of waffles onto the table. She had lost her appetite.

They all agreed to go see the funky chicken. They were prepared to have to fight the Power Outlaws.

They were wrong.

When they arrived in Cragglyville, the funky chicken was still there dancing. And like Spencer had predicted, a crowd of townspeople had gathered. People were clapping and cheering it on as it moved and grooved and jived. They probably thought it was just a guy in a suit. Nikki looked around—she didn't see the Power Outlaws.

58

Mike and Freddy flanked her. They were all wearing their superhero costumes. The sidekicks were hiding somewhere, just in case they were needed. No one noticed Nikki and her friends as they walked right up to where the chicken was performing. They were too busy watching the chicken dance.

Nikki spotted a policewoman who was standing on the outskirts of the crowd. She approached her. "Excuse me, officer," Nikki said politely.

The woman turned to see who had addressed her. Nikki expected her to be surprised, to say something like, "Oh my gosh, Nikki Powergloves? What are you doing here?" Instead, the lady smiled at her. It was not a friendly smile. It was cold and hard. Nikki thought it looked evil. The woman said, "What can I do for you, young lady?"

Although she was unsettled by the woman's strange reaction, Nikki didn't know what else to do so she plowed right ahead. "I, uh, we, um, we need to get all these people out of here right now!"

The woman nodded and smiled again. Her face was cold and uncaring. "Yes, we do," she said, as if she knew that Jimmy Powerboots was about to fire a hundred missiles at the exact spot they were standing on. The policewoman raised a radio to her lips and said, "They're here." Then she smiled for a third time.

Nikki ran. She pulled Mike and Freddy behind her. Somehow she sensed the attack was coming, and she knew it wasn't Naomi or any of the other Power Outlaws. And it wasn't aimed at the people of Cragglyville. The funky chicken was a trap, yes, but it was a trap for them—for the Power Council. And she already knew who was behind it: the Power Trappers!

Someone screamed. Someone in the crowd. Nikki whirled around. A gap had opened up in the throng of people. Men, women and children were backing away from something, allowing it to pass. The funky chicken. Except it was no longer funky. It stomped right past the onlookers, without so much as a wiggle or a thrust or a spin. No longer dancing—it was hunting. And they were the prey.

As the chicken approached, Nikki felt a gust of air from above her at the same time she heard the roar of an engine. Keeping one eye on the chicken, she cocked her head to look in the air. Three black helicopters were roaming the sky above them. STING copters. As Nikki had guessed, the whole funky chicken charade had been a trap set by the Power Trappers.

The big chicken was about two steps away from them. Freddy stepped in front of Nikki and Mike protectively. He was wearing a purple sock and a black sock. The purple one had a picture of a microphone on it. Nikki had never seen him use that one. The black sock had a picture of a pair of nunchucks on it. It gave Freddy ninja skills.

Freddy spoke. He said, "Hey, funky chicken! STOP!" Nikki could see that it was Freddy who spoke, but it wasn't his voice. It was her dad's voice. Freddy sounded just like her dad. It was the weirdest thing. But it worked.

The chicken stopped cold. It was staring at Freddy, making weird squawking sounds. It seemed to be confused.

Freddy spoke again, sounding just like Mr. Nickerson: "Come closer, funky chicken."

Obediently, the chicken took two steps forward, until it was right in front of Freddy. With a loud, "Hiyah!" Freddy whipped a wicked roundhouse kick across the chicken's wing. The wing cracked and broke away from the chicken's body. Nikki was shocked to see what was uncovered.

Red and blue wires dangled from the chicken. They were sparking and crackling with electricity. Inside the hole that Freddy had made, Nikki could see shards of metal and rough green circuit boards. The funky chicken was a robot!

And the robot chicken was angry. It seemed to realize that Freddy had tricked it. With a loud *Squawk!* the chicken aimed a clawed foot at Freddy's head. *Thwop!* The kick connected, knocking Freddy backwards and into Nikki and Mike, who were flattened by his big body.

They rolled across the cement in a tangle of arms and legs. Nikki's arm scraped on the ground. When she stopped moving, she looked at her scraped arm. It stung. A thin sheet of red blood was starting to ooze out. She didn't have time to think about it though. Instead, she scrambled to her feet and extended one hand to Mike and one to Freddy. She easily pulled them back onto their feet, like they weighed no more than a feather each. She was wearing her purple glove, which gave her super-strength.

She pushed Freddy and Mike behind her and turned to face the funky chicken. It was clucking and stomping toward them, looking deranged with only one wing. Its eyes were bugged out and scary-looking. Nikki took one step toward it and then *POW!* she clocked it with a big punch. The chicken went flying about thirty feet and then crunched onto the sidewalk, leaving a trail of metal gears, colored wires, and shiny parts. The chicken was completely destroyed.

But the black helicopters were still circling them, moving closer and closer. Somehow Nikki knew that the parachuting Weebles were not going to be able to save them this time.

One of the copters buzzed past her and Nikki could see one of the big, burly men from the cabin hanging out of the door. Nikki expected him to have a net-shooting gun again, but his hands were empty. There was something at his feet. It was round and metallic and glinted whenever a ray of sunlight reflected off of it. About the size of a basketball, the thing had three-foot-long wings extended on either side of it.

The man kicked the ball out of the helicopter. From its trajectory, Nikki could tell it would fall well short of where her and her friends were standing. But it didn't. The wings began flapping and the ball headed straight for them. "Down!" Nikki yelled, as she threw herself flat on her stomach.

The winged ball *whooshed* past, nearly hitting Nikki in the head. She looked around her and, thankfully, Mike and Freddy had been as fast as she had been. Nikki craned her neck and watched as the other two

STING helicopters tore past. Each had a big guy standing at the doorway. And each big guy kicked a winged ball out the door.

"Incoming!" Nikki yelled. She took off, running as fast as she could. And she was really fast, because in addition to her purple glove, she was wearing her orange glove with the picture of the shoes on it. "Super-speed!" she yelled as she ran along, moving so fast that someone watching would barely be able to see her. She was just a blur as she sprinted up the road. She had to hope that the others would find a way to run from the winged basketballs, too.

When she felt she was far enough away, she slowed down to a walk and turned around to see where Mike and Freddy were. Immediately she spotted Mike, who had used his black scarf to turn his body to rubber. He was bouncing along the street as one of the balls chased him. Freddy was further down the street, using his ninja skills to flip away from the other two balls. He was fast, but not fast enough, as one of the balls managed to slam into him, knocking him flat on his back. Strangely, the ball seemed to stick to him, like metal on a magnet. Freddy tried to stand up, but couldn't. The ball was weighing him down.

One of the copters moved toward him and three big men swung out of the door on long rope ladders. The helicopter moved them close enough to the ground for them to scramble down the ladders and drop to the street level. They ran straight toward Freddy!

Nikki ran harder than she had ever run. Her legs were pumping so fast she wasn't even sure they were there anymore. Her arms moved rapidly, too, like a machine, pumping at her sides. She reached Freddy before the big men, and stood over him, protectively.

The men stopped to look at her. One of them had a huge neck as big as his head. He said, "We're going to have to take you both in."

"Not happening," Nikki said. She glared at the men. The one with the big neck took a step toward her. He pulled a big gun out of his hip holster. The other two men did the same thing. Three guns. All aimed right at Nikki. They couldn't all miss her. One of them would catch her in the net.

Behind the men, Nikki saw Mike bounce one more time and then get hit by the flying ball that was chasing him. It stuck to his rubbery chest, pinning him to the ground. The third flying ball zipped past Nikki and then circled around, locking in on where she was standing. Three net guns and one flying ball, all with one goal: to capture her. She was in big trouble.

Then the sidekicks arrived.

They popped up out of nowhere, on all sides of Nikki. Spencer had his black sunglasses on and a huge grin on his face. They were all carrying egg-shaped objects. "Rainbow Fog!" Spencer yelled. Spencer, Dexter and Chilly began tossing the eggs, which were really grenades, in every direction. They clinked along the street and sidewalks. *Clink, clink*: one landed at the feet of the guy with the big neck. *Clink, clink*: one bounced past Nikki. A few dozen more clinks and the grenades were all over the place, some wedged in cracks in the ground and others rolling and spinning across the pavement.

Nikki counted to three before springing into action. Right when she said *Three!* in her mind, she grabbed Freddy under her arm and started running toward Mike. Her timing was perfect. The grenades went off, sending streams of colorful mist in all directions. With the number of grenades that the sidekicks had thrown, the entire street was soon coated in a thick layer of multi-colored fog.

Nikki reached Mike and could barely see him through the mist. Like Freddy, she tucked him under her arm. Her other arm. Now she had one power kid under each arm, each with a weird flying basketball magnet thing stuck to them. And the flying basketballs were heavy! Even with her super-strength, Nikki had to strain to carry them.

Next she sprinted in a circle, aiming for the approximate spots where she had last seen the sidekicks. The first one she found was Chilly. In fact, she slammed right into her, knocking her over. "Oomf!" Chilly said.

"Sorry," Nikki said. "We don't have much time. Climb on!" Chilly got back on her feet and clambered up Nikki's back and onto her shoulders.

Nikki headed for where she thought Dexter was. The fog was as thick as molasses, preventing Nikki from seeing anything at all. She could hear the helicopters buzzing overhead, but they sounded farther away now. They had probably rose high into the air when the Rainbow Fog appeared.

"Dexter!" Nikki hissed.

"I'm here," she heard a tiny voice say. It wasn't too far from her. She probed her hands forward in the darkness until she felt a body.

"Eek!" Dexter said.

"It's me—Nikki," Nikki said. "Climb on."

Like Chilly, Dexter climbed up Nikki's back like a monkey. He wrapped his arms around Chilly's neck. Chilly had her arms wrapped around Nikki's neck. Nikki was now carrying four kids—Freddy and Mike under her arms and Chilly and Dexter on her back. One more kid to find: Spencer.

Rather than clearing, the fog seemed to be getting even thicker, like it had graduated from molasses to pea soup. While searching for the other four members of the Power Council, Nikki had become disoriented, unsure of where she was or where Spencer might be. She was about to yell Spencer's name when she heard a voice cry, "Polo!" It was Spencer's voice, and Nikki couldn't help but to laugh. Here they were, lost in a swirly Rainbow Fog, surrounded by power Trappers, and her best friend wanted to play *Marco/Polo*.

"Marco!" Nikki yelled, moving in the direction she had last heard Spencer's voice.

"Polo!" Spencer yelled. She was getting closer to his voice. *WHAM!* Nikki felt like she had bumped into a brick wall. Her head ached from the collision. While balancing Freddy under her arm, she reached out with her hand and felt a big, muscly leg. Not a wall, a man. A big man. A Power Trapper!

She felt a strong arm try to grab her, but she managed to kick at it, knocking it away from her. The man grunted in pain. Nikki's super-strength had been felt by her attacker. She ran in the opposite direction, then turned sharply to the right, ran a few more feet, and turned right again. She was headed back in Spencer's direction, but far enough away from where she had run into the Power Trapper.

She took a risk and yelled, "Marco!" and to her surprise, Spencer shouted, "Polo!" from practically right in her ear. He was next to her, moving in the opposite direction.

"Hurry," Nikki said. "Climb on, Spence!"

Finally, the colorful mist was beginning to clear. Nikki could see Spencer's toothy grin. He said, "Okay, Jungle-Gym," and pulled himself up onto Nikki's back. Nikki wobbled a little as she felt the effect of having three kids stacked on her shoulders, but she managed to steady herself enough to start running, using her super-speed to propel her down the street.

The three big Power Trappers were blocking her escape.

She swerved sharply around the first one, leaving him clutching at empty air. The second guy dove at her feet but she was moving so fast that he accidentally tackled a fire hydrant instead. The last Power Trapper just tried to get in her way, so she leapt high in the air, easily clearing his head.

The STING helicopters were still hovering in the air above her, but Nikki knew they wouldn't be able to keep up with her super-speed. She was home free!

She ran all the way back to the Power City without stopping.

10

The Great Weeble comes forward

They were back in the Power City. Nikki was massaging her sore arms and legs. Carrying five kids was hard work. Even with super-strength.

She had used her last ounces of strength to pull the magnet balls off of her friends. Later they would be taken to the sidekicks' Lab for research.

"We sure showed those Power Trappers that they can't mess with us! Kapow!" Spencer said excitedly.

"We all did well," Nikki said. "Especially the sidekicks. Without that Rainbow Fog we might not have made it."

Everyone was happy and safe, but Nikki was worried. How were they supposed to rescue Samantha when they were too busy trying to not get captured by the Power Trappers? She needed help. They all needed help. "We need help," Nikki said.

"Do you want to go talk to the Monkey's Uncle?" Freddy suggested.

Nikki thought about it. The last time she had spoken to the wise, old monkey who called himself the Monkey's Uncle, Nikki had felt more confident afterwards. "Maybe," Nikki said.

Mike said, "Or we could request to speak to the Great Weeble?"

"Who's the Great Weeble?" Nikki asked. She had taken a tour of Weebleville, but no one had said anything about a Great Weeble.

"Well, to be honest, none of us really know," Mike replied. "You know how we told you about all the rules the Weebles gave us when they moved into the Power City?"

Nikki nodded. "Sure. One—don't pet the Weebles; two—never accuse a Weeble of lying because they only tell the truth; and three—don't feed the Weebles after midnight."

"Yeah, I learned about the third rule the hard way," Spencer said sheepishly.

"Right," Mike said. "But the rules weren't the only thing they told us. They told us one other thing."

"What?" Spencer asked. He was leaning forward in his seat. Clearly his interest had been piqued. He loved learning new things.

Mike said, "The Weebles told us that at the time when we needed it most, the Great Weeble would tell us great and amazing things."

"Who's the Great Weeble?" Nikki asked again.

Mike shrugged. "I dunno. We've asked to speak to the Great Weeble twice, but both times we were denied. The other Weebles said it wasn't the right time. But maybe now is the right time."

Nikki thought about it and then said, "What do you think, Spence?"

"Let's go for it, Captain-Kangaroo!"

Nikki laughed. "Okay. We're going to Weebleville."

Ten minutes later they were standing in front of a huge iron door. The sign above the door said, "Weebleville." It was written in shaky, childish handwriting. Mike and Freddy each put a hand on the door handle and pulled with all of their might. The door groaned and slowly opened. Nikki slipped through the opening first, with Spencer and the other sidekicks right behind her.

Inside the door there was chaos!

Which was normal for Weebleville. Blaring carnival music could be heard coming from the city. There were rows of houses lining the streets but Nikki didn't think the Weebles actually used them for sleeping or living. Because she never actually saw the Weebles go inside of them. They were more like props for their games.

The first Weeble she spotted was light blue, with long bristles that had been flattened onto his back. He was running and laughing. "Hoo hoo hoo," he giggled. Soon Nikki realized that he wasn't actually colored blue. On his belly she could see grayish fur, with specks of white mixed in. He was being chased by a yellow Weeble holding a spatula and a tub of something blue. The spatula was covered in blue goo from the tub. Nikki immediately recognized what it was: hair gel. A few months earlier, Spencer had decided that he needed to "style" his hair, so he bought a tub of similar blue goo. The next day he came to school with his new hairdo. His blond locks were slicked back. It didn't look good. His hair just looked wet. He never used the blue hair gel ever again.

The Weeble with the spatula and the blue goo leapt at the other Weeble from behind and tackled him. They rolled and rolled and rolled and when they stopped, the tub of gel was empty and they were both covered in blue goo. Nikki started laughing so hard her sides began to shake. The rest of her friends were laughing too. The Weebles were always good for a laugh. They were very funny, a little bit crazy, a lot kooky, and even somewhat loony. Not to mention zany, and bonkers, and nutty. In fact, if they ever invented a candy bar called a Weeble, it would have to be full of nuts.

Finally the kids stopped laughing, and Nikki said, "Which Weeble do we talk to?"

"I think any of them," Mike said. "But maybe *not* the ones covered in goo."

Nikki giggled. She started looking for another Weeble to talk to. They were everywhere, as usual. Running around, making weird noises and doing weird things. Like setting off fireworks under their own butts. Or tying each other up. Or hang gliding off of the houses. To them, all these crazy activities were fun. It's what they liked to do.

None of them looked like they wanted to stop playing to talk to a bunch of kids.

Nikki tried to find one who was at least not moving very much. She spotted a small, black Weeble who was staying in once place. He was trying to crawl into a big, poofy, white dress. It looked like a wedding gown. Nikki approached him.

"Are you getting married or something?" she asked him.

The Weeble looked at her strangely. "Eh, what's it to you, kid?"

"If you *are* getting married, I don't want to distract you on such an important day."

"Nah," the Weeble said, "I just felt like getting dressed up today, is that alright with you?"

Nikki giggled. "But you're a boy. And that is a dress."

"So?" the Weeble said. "A guy can wear a dress. Haven't you ever seen those Scottish guys with the bagpipes? They wear dresses."

Spencer said, "Actually, they're called kilts. And they're more like skirts than dresses."

The Weeble glared at Spencer. "Who are you? The fashion police?"

"No, I'm the boy who fed a Weeble after midnight," Spencer said proudly.

The Weeble's face lit up into a smile. "No way! You're famous, kid. All the Weebles have been talking about you since that night." He lowered his voice and said, "Think you can feed me after midnight next time?"

Spencer laughed. "Sorry, but I can't. You Weebles are hard enough to handle when you're small size."

"Hey, who you callin' small, pipsqueak? Your girlfriend here is bigger than you are!"

Spencer's faced turned red. Nikki said, "C'mon, guys, we're not here to talk about all this. We have a favor to ask you, Mr. Weeble."

The Weeble finished pulling the dress over his plump, round body. It was way too big for him. He looked like he was drowning in all the

69

lace, frills, and bows. Nikki wondered where he could have possibly found the dress. She tried not to laugh.

The Weeble said, "Okay, okay, what's the favor?"

"We want to speak to the Great Weeble," Nikki declared.

"Is that right?" the Weeble said. "Take a number because you could be waiting a while. Everyone wants to talk to the Great Weeble, but he doesn't want to talk to anyone right now."

Nikki put her hands together like she was praying. "Please, please, please, Mr. Weeble. Can you just ask him?"

"Geez, you're pushy, kid. If you stop calling me *Mr. Weeble*, then I'll help you. Name's Roy."

"Thank you, Mr. Wee—I mean, Roy."

"Whatever, kid. Follow me." Roy rolled off down the road and within minutes, his clean, white dress was dirty and littered with rocks. Nikki and her friends raced after him, passing dozens of Weebles who continued to play and have fun as if the kids weren't even there.

Eventually the Weeble stopped rolling. They were in front of a huge, stone tower. "Wait here," he said. He left them and rolled through a circular opening in the stone blocks. While she was waiting, Nikki wondered to herself what the Great Weeble would look like. She pictured him as an extra big, extra round old Weeble, with gray and white bristles. He would be well-educated and not silly or goofy like the rest of the Weebles. Surely, he would be able to help them. Nikki soon found out that she was both right and wrong.

Eventually the Weeble in the wedding dress scampered out of the tower and said, "It's your lucky day, kid. The Great Weeble will see you now." Nikki's heart leapt! Finally the power kids would be able to meet the greatest Weeble of all.

With a quick, "Thanks, Roy," Nikki ran past the Weeble and into the tower. A long gray banner read, "Welcome to Weeble Tower," in large white letters. Past the sign was a winding stone staircase.

Nikki led her friends under the banner to the stairs. She paused at the foot of the staircase. "Only place to go is up," she said. Mike shrugged and motioned for her to lead.

They started up the stairs. Somewhere behind her, Spencer was counting the steps. "One stippy, steppy, stappy. Two stippy steppy stappies. Three…" he said. Ten minutes later they were still climbing and Spencer was still counting, although he had shortened his phrase. "Five hundred and thirty two stip, step, stap," he said. There was no end in sight. From the street it hadn't looked like the tower was *this* tall. She wondered if the staircase was magical.

When Spencer's count reached nine hundred and eighty, Nikki thought she could see the end of the staircase. Twenty stippy steppy stappies later, Nikki reached a small wooden door. "One thousand stippila, steppila, stappilas!" Spencer exclaimed.

"Good job, everyone," Nikki said. They were all breathing hard, panting to try to catch their breaths. Nikki's legs were already sore after their narrow escape from the Power Trappers, but now they were on fire from the climb. Being a superhero was not all fun and games— sometimes it was really hard work.

When they were all breathing normally again, Nikki knocked on the door. *Thud, thud, thud!* Her knocks echoed down the stairwell, bouncing off the stone walls and fading into the distance.

She heard a voice behind the door say, "C'mon in, ya'll!"

When Nikki looked at her other friends they just shrugged, so she pushed the door open. It creaked slightly as it arced into the room. Nikki glanced around the space. It was perfectly circular, with a stone floor and stone walls. Against the wall was a huge gold throne with a plush, red velvet cushion on the seat. The room was empty.

Nikki frowned and looked back at Spencer, who had entered behind her. "There's no one here," she said.

Spencer started humming to himself softly, a sign that he was thinking. Nikki's eyes followed her friend's gaze as he looked upwards, as if he expected the Great Weeble to be levitating in the air. The ceiling was high above them. Chained to the ceiling was a large, bright chandelier. It looked expensive.

Spencer lowered his gaze and said, "We heard a voice and there's no way out of this tower except down the stairs. Which means that whoever spoke through the door is still here."

Nikki knew her friend's logic made sense, but it didn't explain where the Weeble had gone. She shrugged. Spencer looked at her with a mischievous grin on his face and then began walking casually toward the throne. He said, "I think we've probably all been assuming that the Great Weeble would be great in both mind *and* body. In other words, we all thought he would be the biggest Weeble we'd ever seen, excluding the poor Weeble that partook of the little midnight snack I prepared the other day. But we were all wrong." Spencer took a few more steps, until he was standing next to the throne. He bent down and grasped a piece of red velvet cloth that ran from the seat of the chair down to the floor. Looking back at Nikki, he said, "In fact, the Great Weeble might be the smallest Weeble we have ever seen!" With a flourish, he flung the cloth upwards.

"Ooohoohoohoo, oohoohoo!" the small ball of fur laughed, as it rolled out from underneath the throne. It moved unimaginably fast, spinning circles around Spencer and then around Nikki. It bounced off of one wall and then scampered across and bounced off of another wall. It hopped on one leg and then on the other leg. All in all, it was putting on quite a show. And the entire time it was laughing like a maniac, sometimes high-pitched and squeaky—*hee hee hee hoo hoo hee hee ha!*—and sometimes low and sinister—*Mwah ha ha ha!*

Nikki watched as its crazy antics continued for a few more minutes. Normally she would have laughed, but she couldn't stop thinking *This crazy nutter is the Great Weeble?*

Spencer, on the other hand, was laughing so hard that no sound was coming from his lips. His mouth was wide open, his head was shaking, and he was holding his stomach.

Finally the bristly animal performed a flip, a spin, and one more flop, and then hopped up on his throne, resting his butt on the velvet pillow. "Whatcha can I do ya for?" he said, looking right at Nikki. Unlike the other Weebles, he did *not* have a New York accent. But he did have an accent. It sounded sort of country-ish, like some of the farmers that lived in Cragglyville talked.

Spencer looked at Nikki, but she didn't know what to say. She barely understood the Weeble's question. Seeming to realize Nikki's difficulty, Spencer turned to face the Weeble and said, "Great Weeble, thank you for letting us come to speak with you."

"Ain't no trouble at all," the Great Weeble said. And then: "Come closer, y'all, so I can see yer faces."

Nikki and her friends moved forward to stand in a line next to Spencer. The Weeble spoke again. "Lemme guess. Y'all want advice about somethin'?"

Spencer said, "Yessir. You see, we've got these really nasty dudes chasing us, they call themselves the Power Trappers. We don't know how to beat them."

The Great Weeble leaned his head back and looked at the chandelier above them. "Ahhhhh," he sighed. "I see yer predickyment. I ain't sure if I can help, but I've got plenty to tell y'all."

"What do you have to tell us?" Nikki blurted out.

"Ahh, the temporary leader of the Power Council speaks at last," the Great Weeble said. "I know things thatcha need to know, but I couldn't tell ya until now. Great things. Perhaps I should start from the beginning." The small Weeble motioned a paw to the floor, indicating that the kids should sit down. Obediently, Nikki sat cross-legged on the cold floor.

Once they were all situated, the Great Weeble spoke again. "Many years ago the Power Giver discovered one hundred and forty four powers—"

"Who's the Power Giver?" Spencer asked.

"Ahh, you must be the curious one—the one they say is a genius," the Great Weeble said.

"That's me, Spencer Quick, certified genius."

"Well, son, yer just gonna have to live with not havin' all the answers right now. Can ya do that?"

A look of pain crossed Spencer's face. Nikki knew that he hated not knowing the answer to something. He grimaced, like someone had punched him in the stomach, but then nodded his head and said, "I think so, Great Weeble, sir."

"Good, now where was I. Ahh, yes, the Power Giver. So he found these incredible powers. Powers that made 'im fly and talk to animals and such." Spencer squirmed in his seat. Nikki could tell he wanted to ask another question but was trying to restrain himself. To be honest, Nikki had a few questions of her own. Like where did the Power Giver find these powers? And what did they look like? But she kept her mouth shut and continued to listen to the Great Weeble.

The Great Weeble said, "The Power Giver has been secretly usin' his powers ter help folks fer a long time. If I'm bein' honest, he's gettin' old. The powers allow 'im ter do a lot of things, but he can't cheat death, no sirey, no one can do that. He needed ter pass his powers along, and he ain't got no family and he don't trust the adults, so he picked the kids. He picked all of you."

Nikki was astonished. She had somehow been *chosen* by the Power Giver—whoever he was—to receive her powergloves! But how?

The Weeble said, "I'm sure y'all have a lot of questions, but I ain't gonna answer 'em. I'll only say what I'll say. And the last thing y'all need to know is that yer powers will only last until yer next birthday."

"August 25th?" Nikki said.

"How'd you know my birthday, Nikki?" Mike said.

"*You're* birthday?" Nikki said. "That's *my* birthday."

"Wait, guys, are you joking around? That's *my* birthday," Freddy said.

Spencer raised a hand to get everyone's attention. "Oh yeah, this is getting better every day. Don't you see? You all have the same birthday. And I'll bet a midnight Weeble snack that Samantha *and* the Power Outlaws have the same birthday, too."

Nikki, Mike and Freddy looked at each other, their eyes widening in surprise.

The Great Weeble said, "Yer friend here is smart, real smart. And he's right. The powers will only last until August 25th, and then they *might* just vanish in the blink of an eye." The Great Weeble winked at Nikki. He had a twinkle in his gray eyes and a slight grin on his face.

"They *might* vanish?" Spencer asked. "Do you mean there is a way to stop the powers from disappearing?"

"Hoo hoo hoo hoo!" the Great Weeble giggled. "You are smart indeed, young Jedi, but I can't answer any more questions. It's time fer y'all to go!" With that, the Great Weeble leapt from his cushion and began bouncing around the room, laughing and giggling wildly. With a final bounce, he sprang out the door and down the stairs, leaving Nikki and her friends puzzling over what he had told them.

11

Gnomes: more than just good gardeners

After leaving Weeble Tower, Nikki and her friends made their way back through Weebleville. They had almost reached the door out of the city when they heard a voice from behind.

"Yo, Nikki," the voice said.

Nikki turned to see the Weeble wearing the wedding dress. The material was brown and tattered and singed and wet, like it had recently been set on fire and then extinguished with a bucket of water.

Nikki said, "Hi, Roy. Thanks again. Our talk with the Great Weeble was interesting."

"I think I can help you," Roy the Weeble said.

"Help us what?" Nikki asked.

"Defeat the Power Trappers." Roy had flipped over and was standing on his head as he spoke. He couldn't seem to stand still.

"How do you know about the Power Trappers?" Nikki asked.

Roy had started chasing his broad, flat tail. Each time he turned he said another few words. "We all know...much more than you...might think," he said.

"Okay," Nikki said. "How can you help?"

"I've got some friends..."

"More Weebles?" Spencer interrupted.

"No, different kinds of friends," Roy said cryptically. "Follow me."

He led them down a side street past a row of houses. They saw a few Weebles playing, but not nearly as many as they had seen on the main street that ran through Weebleville. On the right a bright orange Weeble was launching apples at a brown Weeble who was trying to catch them in his mouth. On the left Nikki saw a dark black Weeble doing the hula hoop. But not just one hoop; she had at least a dozen hoops spinning around her chubby body at the same time! Nikki giggled. Although the Weebles were strange, they were talented—in their own way.

They followed Roy for another few blocks until he approached one of the houses. It was red brick with yellow shutters and black shingles. He opened the blue front door without a key.

"Is this your house?" Spencer asked curiously.

"Nah, I don't know whose it is," Roy said. "But I know where it leads."

Nikki didn't understand what he meant. How could the house lead anywhere? A house was a destination, not a road. She remembered the three Weeble rules. One of the rules was that Weebles could not tell a lie. She knew she had to trust Roy, so she kept following him.

The inside of the house looked nothing like the outside. The outside looked normal, but as Spencer would say, the inside was *crazytown*. There were big brightly colored rubber balls all over the place. Black lights illuminated everything, making things look eerie and mystical. Nikki looked at Spencer, who was grinning. His teeth looked bright white and shiny because of the black light on his braces. His face was purple! He looked hilarious! Nikki started laughing and soon all of her friends were chuckling along with her. Roy was laughing, too. As he laughed, he rolled around, bouncing off the bright balls and knocking them around the room.

Eventually he stopped and said, "That was fun, but we better move on." He rolled down a hallway to an inner door. When he opened the door, dark gloom spilled out.

"Be careful," Roy said. "We have to go down the steps." And then he plunged into the darkness.

Nikki paused on the threshold. Looking back at Spencer, she said, "What do you think?"

Spencer said, "I trust him, Little-Orphan-Annie."

"Okay, here goes nothing," Nikki said, before stepping into the gloom. At first her foot hung awkwardly in the air, but then she felt it reach solid ground. The first step. She probed with her arms to the sides, trying to locate a handrail. She felt only a rough wall. Running her hands along the walls, she made her way down the staircase. She had no idea how far Roy was in front of her, or how far Spencer was behind her.

After descending at least fifty steps, Nikki said, "Spencer, you there?"

Spencer said, "This is one scary place. I can't see a thing!" His voice was pretty close behind her. "Hey, Freddy! Did you dig this tunnel for Roy?"

Freddy's voice answered but it sounded a lot further away than Spencer's. "No, I don't know who dug it."

Spencer said, "Well, it couldn't have been Roy, he doesn't even have hands!"

"Hey, I heard that!" Roy said from somewhere in front of Nikki. "Weebles may not have hands, but our paws are remarkably dexterous." Nikki found it strange to be having a conversation with her friends and a Weeble, while walking down a staircase in complete darkness.

Roy said, "If you must know, my friends dug the tunnel. Be careful here, the steps are ending." Nikki heard the Weeble scraping and shuffling ahead of her.

She slowed down slightly as she dropped down a final step, and then she was walking on a flat path. It was still pitch dark. The ground beneath her felt soft and earthy. The kids and Roy walked in silence as they went up a rise and then down the other side. Another rise. Another downslope. Suddenly the air didn't seem as thick. It was still dark, but Nikki thought she could make out the outline of the ball of fur shuffling along in front of her. She waved a hand in front of her face and saw it flash past her field of vision. The tunnel was getting lighter. Nikki glanced back and saw her friends striding behind her. They were spread out a safe distance to prevent themselves from crashing into each other in the dark. Spencer grinned at her.

"I wonder what kind of friends a Weeble has," Spencer whispered.

Nikki shrugged and said, "Probably not humans." She was kind of joking but didn't realize how right she was.

Soon the tunnel ended and Roy stopped. In front of him was a thick patch of green shrubs and vines. The light was coming through cracks in the leaves. "Welcome to the Gnome Gardens," Roy said. He pushed through the greenery.

Nikki followed behind him and held the vines and branches for Spencer, before looking outside. For a moment she was blinded. The sun was shining brightly and she had been walking in darkness for so long that he eyes weren't used to the light. It was like going to see a movie in the early afternoon and coming out to a sunny day.

She squinted to let her eyes adjust to the light. Little by little, she lifted her eyelids until her eyes were fully open. Her vision was blurry at first but then began to clear. As it did, her mouth popped open in astonishment.

In front of her was the most beautiful garden she had ever seen. It looked like it belonged in some magical fairytale land with princesses and knights and dwarfs. But it was real. She touched the petals of an enormous flower that was growing next to the tunnel entrance. The petals felt like silk. They were vibrant purple with speckles of yellow. The light green leaves were so waxy they looked fake. The flower looked so happy in the garden that it was almost smiling. In fact, all the flowers she could see looked happy. There were perfectly shaped yellow and red tulips, exquisite red and white rosebushes, breathtaking fields of white orchids, and a hundred other kinds of flowers that Nikki didn't know the names of. Each plant in the garden was meticulously pruned. There were no weeds or stray tufts of grass growing anywhere. *The garden must have very good gardeners*, Nikki thought.

Roy had moved down a lovely, white-stone garden path. He turned to face Nikki. "What do you think?"

"It's incredible," Nikki cooed. "Thank you for bringing us, Roy."

Roy looked embarrassed but Nikki could tell he was pleased. He spun around awkwardly and rolled into the gardens. Nikki waited for her friends, who had all exited the tunnel. Their reactions were similar to hers. Spencer started spouting all kinds of crazy words, like *Poppy-Magical!* and *Tooberrific!* while the other kids used more standard words of appreciation, such as *Amazing* and *Beautiful*, to describe the garden.

Nikki and Spencer walked side by side at the front, trying to catch up to Roy the Weeble. They found him lying on a wide circle of grass set within the garden. His fur was sticking in all directions and had bits of grass stuck between his bristles, like he had just rolled around on the lawn.

But what really caught Nikki's attention were the dozens of statues that stood on the grass around him. Gnomes. Dozens of gnome statues were fixed in various positions. They all wore hats with wide brims, as if they were worried about getting sunburned. The male gnomes had thick, gray beards that looked almost lifelike. The women wore long, bright dresses that covered their feet.

They were all made to look like they were working. Some had shovels and trowels, while others held tiny clippers and combs. There were gnomes with burlap sacks and gnomes with handfuls of fertilizer.

Then Nikki noticed the gnome statues throughout the rest of the garden. They were everywhere. Between rows of flowers and underneath trees. On ladders and lying on their bellies. It was the most intricate display of garden gnomes Nikki had ever seen. In fact, she had only seen one garden gnome before: a small hand-carved statue that Farmer Miller kept in his herb garden to keep the rabbits away.

"Say hello to my friends," Roy said.

Nikki laughed. "Where?" she asked.

Roy looked at her strangely. He waved his paw in a circle. "All around you. The gnomes."

Nikki frowned. Her first thought was, *Poor Roy here has lost his marbles. He's making friends with inanimate objects.* But then one of the gnomes moved. Not like a gust of wind made it twitch slightly or an earthquake made it wobble. It actually moved on its own.

The gnome walked straight up to Nikki with short, shuffling strides. He was about as tall as her knee. With a graceful sweep of his hand, he removed his hat and bowed deeply. "It is a pleasure to meet you, Princess Nikki Powergloves," the gnome said. Nikki was so astonished that the gnome was actually moving that she barely heard what he had said.

Spencer, however, heard every word. He snorted and snickered. "Princess? Nikki's no princess, I can promise you that."

Nikki glared at her friend and finally remembered her manners. "Thank you, dear gnome. I have to apologize for my friend's behavior. You see, we're not used to meeting gnomes every day. But my friend is right, I'm not a princess."

The gnome was still bowing deeply, his hand across his heart. He said, "To us, Nikki, you *are* a princess. All human girls are."

"Does that mean I'm a prince?" Spencer said, grinning.

"Alas, young gentleman, but we in the gnome kingdom value our women as the true treasures that they are. Unfortunately for me, men do not share the same stature."

Nikki already liked the gnomes. If she understood it correctly, girls were princesses and boys were, well, they were just boys. "What is your name?" she asked.

Finally, the gnome rose up from his bow and replaced his brimmed sun hat. Right away, Nikki noticed his eyes. At first she thought they were brown. Then she thought they were blue. Next they looked green. Finally she realized they were all three colors: blue at the top, brown on the bottom, and green along the sides. They looked magical.

The rest of the gnome's features were rather ordinary, with a long gray beard that nearly reached his feet, a mop of thick gray hair that stuck out from under his hat, and a broad face with a round knobby nose.

The gnome said, "My birth name is Charles Badger Cassanova the third, but you can call me Chuck—all my friends do."

"Well, it is very nice to meet you, Chuck," Nikki said. She started to motion to Spencer. "This is—"

"Spencer, Mike, Freddy, Dexter, and Chilly," Chuck the gnome said. "The Power Council. Missing one, Samantha, who has been kidnapped by STING and the Power Trappers."

Nikki's eyes widened. "How do you know so much, Chuck?"

"Kind princess, let's just say we gnomes make it our business to know as much about the going ons in the human world as possible. We are a small people, so we need to know what the big people are doing, as it could cause us problems."

Nikki nodded. "I think I understand." Finally, she pulled her gaze away from Chuck's magical eyes to look around at the other gnomes. "Are they...?" Nikki said.

"Yes," Chuck said, anticipating her question. "They are all real gnomes. My people are just very good at pretending to be statues, so that humans don't find out about us. You've probably seen garden gnome statues before, right?" Nikki nodded. "Most of the ones you've seen are probably just statues, but every once and a while you might find a real gnome hiding in a garden. We can't seem to stay away from plants and flowers and vegetables. We just love being near them, to smell them, to touch them, to see them."

"Your garden is exquisite," Nikki said, trying to use the biggest, most adult word she could think of.

"Thank you, Princess Nikki. We work hard at it. Now, I'll introduce you to the others." He stuck two fingers between his top and bottom teeth and then blew out, whistling loudly. All around her, the garden came to life. The gnomes on the ladders descended. The ones lying or sitting down stood up. Each and every gnome walked to stand next to or behind Chuck.

Most of them stared at Nikki, but it didn't make her uncomfortable. Their faces looked kind and friendly, and she was staring at them, too, because they all had magical eyes like Chuck.

When they were all gathered together, Roy said, "Told ya so."

Nikki laughed. "Sorry I doubted you, Roy."

Then Chuck began introducing each and every gnome to Nikki and the rest of the Power Council. There must have been at least a hundred gnomes. It was like a receiving line at a wedding. Nikki and her friends shook each and every gnome's hand. Nikki stopped trying to remember their names after the first few.

When all the introductions were done, Nikki remembered why they were there. She spoke directly to Chuck, who seemed to be the spokesperson for the gnomes. "Roy told us you might be able to help us take on the Power Trappers," she said.

Chuck smiled. "We have a few ideas," he said.

Over the next ten minutes, Chuck described what his team of gnomes could do to help.

By the end of Chuck's speech, Nikki and her friends were so excited that they were high-fiving and clapping. Spencer said, "I never would have guessed that the garden gnomes were more than just good gardeners."

12

Into the Power Trappers' lair

Nikki was ready. It was time to save Samantha. Freddy and Mike were in position. So were the sidekicks. Nikki didn't know where Chuck and the gnomes were, but she trusted they would do their part.

From where she was hiding, Nikki could see the front door of the cabin. Freddy and Mike were at the opposite end of the clearing; they were peeking out from behind a couple of large oak trees. Out of the corner of her eye, Nikki spotted the sidekicks. They were creeping along the fringe of the forest, Spencer in front, with Dexter and Chilly trailing behind. In their hands were buckets. Nikki knew what was in the buckets. It was all part of the plan to get into the cabin, where they believed Samantha was being held captive.

Nikki's dad's car wasn't parked next to the cabin like before. She was glad about that. It was going to be hard enough to get into the cabin without her dad complicating things.

Spencer and the sidekicks had left the safety of the woods and were moving across the open clearing. They were crouching as they ran, in the hopes that none of the Power Trappers were keeping a very close watch out the cabin windows. They made it to the row of cars and hid behind a big, black truck. Spencer looked toward where Nikki was hiding. She gave him the signal by sticking her thumb in the air. Then she put on her gray invisibility gloves and disappeared.

Now that she was invisible, she didn't need to worry about hiding anymore. She ran out of her hiding spot and toward the cabin. As she ran, she watched as each of the sidekicks emptied their buckets on the ground in front of the cabin. When they finished, they ran back into the forest. The sidekicks' job was done. Nikki remembered when she had first seen Spencer's invention used against the bad guys. He called the gooey liquid *Sticky Situation Glue*, and it was incredible. When Nikki and the Power Council were fighting against the Power Outlaws, Spencer had poured a vial of the super-sticky glue in front of Jimmy Powerboots. He got so stuck he couldn't move at all. Nikki hoped it would work just as well against the Power Trappers.

She made her way to the back of the cabin, careful not to step on any twigs that might crack and make a noise. Like when she had been there before, the window at the back was open a crack. Also like before, the Power Trappers were seated around a long wooden table drinking big mugs of amber liquid. The only difference this time was that Mr. Nickerson wasn't there. The mood seemed less tense, more relaxed. The men were laughing and joking and drinking.

Ducking below the window, Nikki removed her gray gloves and reappeared. She turned to the forest and gave a thumbs up sign to Mike and Freddy. They returned the signal and then they all settled in to wait for the gnomes. Nikki made herself invisible again, just in case. She looked through the window.

They didn't have to wait long. Nikki heard a loud *Thump!* as something heavy hit the side of the cabin, or maybe the door. One of the muscly men said, "What the…?" and stood up.

The other men watched as the guy went to the door. He opened it a crack and peeked out. "What!? That's impossible!" he said.

The other men looked at each other and then said, "What's impossible, Hank?"

Hank looked back at the other Power Trappers and said, "We're under attack."

The other men scrambled out of their chairs and went to join Hank. He opened the door wide so they could all see. "Gnomes," Hank said. "We're under attack by a bunch of gnomes!"

Nikki heard another *thump!* as something hit the cabin. Then she heard *whizzz!* and watched the Power Trappers duck as a round object flew through the doorway and over their heads. *Thwock!* The object hit the inside wall of the cabin and clattered to the floor. It was a stone, very smooth and round, about the size of a baseball. *Thump, thump, thump, thumpety thump thump, Thump, Thump, THUMP!!* A barrage of stones hit the front of the cabin, the last of which sounded more like a boulder than the baseball-sized stone that had come through the door. It must have taken ten dwarves just to lift it. Or maybe they had a boulder launcher they were using. The dwarves were doing their job—that was for sure.

Hank said, "They're only two feet tall, let's take care of them!" The men let out a cheer that was more like a roar, and ran out the front door, two at a time. *Squish, squish, squish.* Nikki started counting the *squishes* she heard. There were ten guys and she counted ten squishes, which was good.

"Hey!!" she heard one of the men yell, "What's happening?!" Nikki smiled. She knew that Spencer's Sticky Situation Glue had worked perfectly again. Just to be sure, she crept around the side and peeked around the corner. First she saw five dwarves, one of whom was Chuck, standing on the lawn. They had slingshots in their hands, which were raised above their heads in celebration. They were cheering at the front door.

Nikki followed their gaze and saw the ten big Power Trappers. They were standing in a huddle, close to each other, all pulling and prying at their legs and feet, trying to get them free of the glue that bound them to the ground. Nikki knew it was no use without Spencer's anti-stick spray. They were going to be stuck for a long time.

Nikki looked back at the dwarves and gave them the thumbs up sign and then remembered she was still invisible. She was about to slip her gloves off when she saw Chuck look directly at her and smile. He raised his hand and lifted his thumb, returning her signal. Nikki's eyes widened as she realized the dwarves could still see her even though she was invisible. She would have to ask Chuck about that later. But now, she needed to continue the mission before any reinforcements arrived at the cabin.

She hustled to the back of the cabin and shouted, "Let's go!" to Mike and Freddy. She waited for them as they slipped from behind the trees and jogged to where she was standing by the cracked window.

"Are we in?" Mike said when they arrived.

"The sidekicks and the gnomes came through for us," Nikki said.

"Yeah!" Freddy said. He pushed hard on the window and forced it upwards. He started to climb through, but Nikki put a hand on his shoulder and stopped him.

"Before we go in, are we all using the best powers for the job?" Nikki asked.

Freddy lifted one leg and then the other to show Nikki his socks. One sock was various shades of camouflage green. The other was black. Nikki had seen him use both of them before. She said, "The camouflage sock so you're hard to see and the black sock for your ninja skills?"

"Yep," Freddy replied.

"Sounds perfect," Nikki said. "How about you, Mike?"

Mike grinned. "I couldn't let you and Freddy be the only ones who are hard to see," he said. He put a hand on his scarf, which was half black and half white, like a ying-yang. "This baby allows me to do this!" He turned his body to the side and vanished into thin air.

"Where'd you go?" Nikki said. In a flash Mike was back, standing in the same place as before. It was like he stepped through a portal from another dimension.

"When I turn sideways I disappear," he said.

"Cool," Nikki said. "Now we're all stealthy! If there are any guards inside, they won't be able to see any of us! Now, for my powers. Of course I will keep one of my gray gloves for invisibility, and I think I will go with a peach glove so I can pretend to be one of the guards if I need to."

With their powers decided, Freddy gave Nikki a boost onto the window sill and she slid down into the room. She cringed as she realized that she had just entered the Power Trappers lair.

13

Finding Axel

Once they were all inside the cabin, Nikki closed the front door. The big guys outside were still yelling for help. But they were in the middle of the woods, so no one was going to hear them.

She turned around to face her friends. "Let's stick together," she said. "We could cover more ground if we split up, but we'll be safer together if there are more Power Trappers inside here."

Mike said, "Okay, let's start by looking for clues as to where they might be keeping Samantha." The kids fanned out and started poking around the cabin. It was pretty small. It was one room, with a couch and a few plush chairs around the fireplace, the big wooden table for eating, and a small kitchen with a refrigerator. Inside the fridge were a bunch of bottles of the amber liquid she had seen the men drinking, as well as a few jugs of milk, some orange juice, and a carton of eggs. The shelves in the kitchen were lined with boxes of cereal, Pop Tarts, potato chips, and pasta.

The rest of the place was remarkably empty. The three kids rejoined as a group by the front door. "Find anything?" Nikki asked. Freddy and

Mike shook their heads. Nikki said, "Me either. Let's check the doors together."

On the edges of the cabin there were three doors. One was the front door and led outside. When Nikki opened the second door, she found that it was just an empty closet. The third door revealed a bathroom with a toilet and a sink. Nothing else.

"Hmm," Nikki said. "No place to go but up, I guess."

Freddy said, "Before we go up, we should go into stealth mode!" Suddenly his body turned to water. At least it looked like it did. Really, he just took on the colors of his surroundings. He was all brown like the wood cabin wall he was standing in front of. As he walked, his skin tone changed to match whatever he was next to. Even his clothes changed color!

Mike turned sideways and disappeared. Nikki used the power of her gray glove to turn herself invisible. It was almost like none of them were even there.

Freddy said, "So that we don't bump into each other, I'll lead the way. Mike, you go second, and Nikki can protect the rear." Nikki agreed. She was happy to have someone else be the leader for a while. Being a leader was hard work!

She could just make out Freddy's camouflaged body as he moved up the stairs. Once she heard Mike's soft footsteps behind him, she followed her friends. They tiptoed up the wooden planks, trying to be as quiet as possible. When they reached the top, they realized that the top floor was one big room, just like the ground floor. There was nowhere to hold Samantha captive. There were, however, dozens of cardboard boxes half-opened, scattered all over the floor.

Mike reappeared and reached into one of the boxes and pulled out a big, black gun. It was almost as big as he was! He aimed it at one of the other boxes and pulled the trigger. *Thwoop......whisk!* A net made of thick rope shot from the end of the gun and captured the box. Mike pressed a button and the rope began to recoil into the gun's nozzle, pulling the box with it.

"Cool! That's what they used to try to catch you," Freddy said to Nikki. Nikki nodded. She remembered being stuck in the netting with Spencer until the Weebles had parachuted in to save them.

Mike tossed the gun back in the box, opened a few others, and then said, "There's nothing here except weapons and equipment," he said.

Nikki tried to think. What was she missing? Samantha couldn't be in STING headquarters in Cragglyville because they had flooded the building and no one had seen her come out. But they had also checked the Power Trappers cabin and couldn't find any sign of her here either. So where was she?

She said, "Let's check downstairs one more time."

Freddy led them downstairs and they split up and began searching the main cabin again. Nothing had changed. Nikki still didn't see any clues about Samantha. Then she heard Freddy say, "I've got it!" Her heart leapt and she rushed to where Freddy's voice had come from. All three of them reappeared at the same time.

Freddy was pointing at the floor. Nikki saw it right away. Three of the floorboards appeared slightly discolored compared to the rest of the flooring. They looked somewhat gray, whereas the rest of the planks were yellowish brown.

"A trapdoor," Nikki said.

"Stealth mode!" Freddy said. They once more hid themselves and then Freddy used the tips of his fingers to pry one of the planks up. Beneath it: darkness…and a ladder. Cool air wafted up through the gap in the floor. With one plank dislodged, Freddy was easily able to remove the other two discolored planks. Evidently, they were going to have to travel in complete darkness once more.

Like before, Freddy went first. His heavy body made each rung of the ladder creak as he lowered himself down. Nikki followed after him. It wasn't far to the bottom, but by the time they reached it, they couldn't see anything.

"We're going to have to hold hands," Nikki said.

She reached forwards and backwards and her fingers found Freddy's and Mike's hands. Freddy tugged on her hand and began pulling her forwards into the darkness. After a few paces he stopped and said, "Dead end. There's a wall here."

"Let me try the other direction," Mike said. He pulled Nikki the opposite way, and Nikki pulled Freddy. Despite how dark it was, Nikki felt relatively safe having Freddy and Mike on either side of her.

This time they guessed the right direction, and after twenty steps Nikki could see a light up ahead. Soon she could see the walls of the tunnel they were walking through. Unlike the rocky tunnels in the Power City, this tunnel was more like a corridor. The walls, floor and ceiling were smooth and man-made. She still couldn't see Mike (because he was walking sideways), Freddy (because he was camouflaged), or even her own arms and legs (because she was invisible), but it was comforting that she could at least see what was in front of her. Nothing was going to jump out of the dark now.

They reached the end of the corridor, where the path took a ninety-degree turn to the left. The ceiling had built-in panels of fluorescent light to illuminate the way forward. Mike stopped just before the end of the corridor and released Nikki's hand. Nikki followed his lead and let go of Freddy's hand. Her hands felt sweaty and ached a little from gripping her friends' hands. All together, they peeked around the corner.

There was a guy sitting in a chair about halfway down the next hallway.

A big guy.

A Power Trapper!

Behind his chair was a door. It was painted gold. Nikki pulled back from the corner and hissed, "That has to be where they're keeping Samantha."

"But how do we get past the guard?" Mike said.

"We could all gang up on him at the same time," Freddy suggested. "My ninja skills could come in handy."

Nikki thought about it and then said, "Why don't we try something a bit more subtle first, and if that doesn't work, we'll use your ninja skills."

The first thing Nikki did was to reappear, effectively turning off her invisibility. Next she used the power of the peach glove. Moments later she looked just like the Power Trapper named Hank, who was stuck in Spencer's glue outside the cabin.

"Okay," she said. Her voice sounded deep and funny. She sounded just like Hank. "You guys stay tight against the wall. Freddy—you can blend in with the wall; Mike—you can stay sideways so the guy won't be able to see you when he comes around the bend. I'll take care of the guard."

Then Nikki took a few steps back into the hall. She glanced at her hands. They were big and hairy. So were her arms and legs. She looked ridiculous! She was glad she wasn't a Power Trapper. Being a superhero was way better.

She started walking down the corridor, stepping down hard so the guard would be able to hear her footsteps. When she turned the corner he was already on his feet. "What's up, Hank?" he said as she approached.

"The guys need you to go upstairs," she said in her deep voice. "Go out the front door, they're all waiting for you there. I'll take your post while you're gone."

"What do they want?" the guy asked.

"Stop asking stupid questions!" Nikki snapped. "You'll find out when you get up there."

The guy's face went red and then he shrugged and started to walk off. Nikki grabbed his arm with her big hand and said, "Wait. How do I get in to see the prisoner?"

The Power Trapper looked at her strangely. "Why would you need to go in there?" he asked.

"I dunno, I probably won't. But the guard should have the keys, right?"

The guy shrugged again. "I guess so," he said. He reached in his pockets and removed a set of three keys and handed them to Nikki, who he thought was Hank.

"Thanks," Nikki mumbled.

The guy turned and walked down the hall and then turned the corner. Nikki held her breath as he passed where her friends were hiding. She didn't hear him trip, or curse, or say anything at all, so she assumed Mike and Freddy had managed to stay out of his way. Three seconds later, they appeared next to her.

"Great job, Nikki," Freddy whispered.

"What are we going to do when the guy sees the other Power Trappers are stuck in the glue?" Mike asked.

"I bet he'll get stuck, too, when he tries to help them," Nikki said. "They won't be able to warn him in time."

"I hope you're right," Mike said.

Nikki dangled the keys from one of her fingers. "Don't worry about that right now. First we have to get Samantha out."

She transformed back into herself, pushed the chair away from the gold door, and then tried one of the keys. It was too big. She tried the next one. It was the right size, but didn't fit the keyhole. The third key went straight into the lock. Nikki turned it and she heard a click. She tried to push the door open, but it was too heavy.

Mike and Freddy moved to her side and started pushing with her. The door slowly eased open. The room was shiny, like jewelry. Everything was painted gold. Someone was inside, sitting with their back against the gold wall.

To Nikki's shock, it wasn't Samantha.

She was so ready to rush in and give her friend a big hug, grab her hand, and lead her away from her awful prison that Nikki couldn't process who she was seeing.

The boy said, "Hey, losers. Who are you?" He had a strong British accent.

At first, Nikki just stared at him. He was wearing ripped jeans and spotless white shoes. His shirt was black, with a picture of some rock band on the front. The shirt was partially obscured by a denim jacket. He had a gold chain with a silver skull hanging from his neck. One of his ears was pierced. The diamond stud sparkled on his earlobe. His hair was messy, but Nikki guessed that was just the way he wore it. Intentionally messy.

"I'm out of here," the kid said, as he started to push past Nikki.

"Wait," she said. "Who are you?"

The kid stopped and said, "Axel. Axel Powerjackets."

Nikki's eyes widened in surprise. "You mean, you're a power kid, too?"

Axel looked at Nikki curiously. "What do you mean, *too?*"

Nikki extended a hand. "I'm Nikki. Nikki Powergloves," she said.

Axel took her hand and shook it. He was staring at her gloves. "You get powers from those?" he asked, gesturing to the gloves.

"Yeah," Nikki said. "You get powers from wearing that jacket?" she asked.

"Yeah," he said.

Freddy said, "Then why didn't you just break out of this place using your powers?"

Axel's eyes flicked toward Mike. "Who's the fat kid?" he said.

Freddy's face twitched, like he had been slapped. His face turned red. Nikki glared at Axel. His tone had been so mean, so condescending. He didn't seem like a nice kid. He seemed more like Naomi and Jimmy and Peter. A bad guy. A future member of the Power Outlaws. She almost wished she hadn't unlocked his door. But she didn't know. She thought it was Samantha's cell.

"He has a name," Nikki said flatly. "And for your information, he is about as powerful as any power kid out there. His name is Freddy Powersocks. And this is Mike Powerscarves," she said, motioning to Mike.

"Heya, fellas," Axel said. "And for *your* information, I couldn't use my powers because of this stupid gold room. It's made from pure gold and for some reason it blocks our powers. Now, like I said before, I'm outta here. Thanks for the help."

Mike and Freddy blocked the doorway. "Not so fast," Mike said.

Axel said, "Get outta my way, boys."

Nikki wedged her way between them before the pushing started. "Hold on, guys. Look, our best chance to get out of here is to work together as a team. Four kids' powers will be better than one. Whaddya say, Axel?"

Axel stared at the ceiling. Then he said, "I'm more of a loner, but I'll make an exception just this once."

Nikki smiled. "Okay. First things first. Where's Samantha?" she asked.

14

Dart guns: better than laser pistols

"Who's Samantha?" Axel asked.

"Our friend. A nine-year-old with powers—like us. She was captured by the same people that kidnapped you."

"I saw a girl," Axel said. "I don't know her name and just caught a quick glimpse when they were bringing me to my cell. I think they caught her first. They put her further inside the tunnel, but I'm not going that way. I'm heading out."

"Trust me, you're not going to get out without our help. There are about a dozen of those Power Trappers upstairs. As soon as you go through the trapdoor they'll just catch you again." Nikki didn't mention that the Power Trappers were stuck to the ground with Spencer's Sticky Situation Glue.

Axel contorted his face in frustration. "Okay, okay. Let's get the Samantha girl and then get outta here!"

"Where are the rest of your jackets?" Nikki asked.

"In the powerchest in my pocket," Axel replied.

"Why did they let you keep them?"

Axel rolled his eyes. "Don't you know anything? Duh, because every time they tried to touch my powerchest they got shocked."

Nikki remembered back to when she had tried to let Spencer use one of her powergloves. He had been shocked, too. Evidently only power kids could touch the powerchests and power objects.

"Okay," Nikki said. "Let's change our powers to the best ones for this mission."

"I'm fine with the one I got on," Axel said, touching a hand to the collar of his jacket.

"What can you do?" Mike asked.

"You'll find out," Axel said.

Nikki said, "I know what I'm going to use." She opened her powerchest and swapped her peach and gray gloves for an orange one and a purple one. "Nothing beats speed and strength," she said.

"We'll see about that," Axel muttered.

Mike opened his powerchest and removed a brown-striped scarf and wrapped it around his neck. "I think my tornado power might come in handy," he said.

Freddy glanced at Axel before opening his powerchest. He thought for a minute and then extracted a gray sock and a green sock. "Green for protection and gray for fun," Freddy said.

Nikki remembered that the green sock gave Freddy a turtle shell that he could protect himself with. She didn't know what the gray sock would do, but she trusted his judgment. "Okay," Nikki said. "Let's go!"

Axel was the first out the door as the others had to close their powerchests and stuff them back in their pockets. Nikki was next out, following Axel closely.

Axel strode down the hallway confidently, as if he were invincible. Nikki half-jogged to keep up with him. She could hear Freddy's heavy footsteps behind her. She was worried they were all making too much noise.

They approached another bend in the passageway, and she expected Axel to slow down and peek around the corner, like she and her friends had done earlier. They didn't know who or what might be around the corner. But Axel didn't slow down. Instead, he turned sharply at the corner. She saw his hand flick up and a gun appeared. He raised it and fired down the hall. *Bizzzzz!*

Nikki rounded the corner to see who he was shooting at. Three hulking guys wearing tank tops were standing across the hall, blocking the path. All three of them were holding pistols.

They fired!

Nikki used every ounce of her super-speed to dive for cover. *Beeooop! Beeooop!* Nikki heard the shots before she saw them, and then the air was filled with yellow, green, and red beams of light. The Power Trappers were using laser guns!

Nikki was lying on the floor, looking up Axel, who was still on his feet. He calmly sidestepped a laser beam and fired his gun again. *Bizzzz!* Nikki could visibly see the projectile as it left his gun's muzzle. It was a long dart with reddish feathers on the tail. *Thwop!* The dart plunged into one of the guy's massive legs.

The Power Trapper looked down at the feathers protruding from his thigh, as if he was surprised at how they had gotten there. Then his eyes rolled back in his head and he fainted, collapsing to the floor with a loud slap. Nikki heard Axel say, "One down."

The remaining two Power Trappers fired again, but their lasers sailed wide, to the left and right of Axel. One of them tilted his laser pistol down slightly, aiming it directly at Nikki's head. She froze.

Bizzzz! Thwop! Axel's dart hit the guy in the shoulder and he slumped to the floor like a sack of potatoes. Axel had just saved Nikki! "Two down, one to go," Axel muttered.

The last Power Trapper wasn't going to go down without a fight. He started firing at Axel wildly. A blue laser cut a hole through the fringe of Axel's powerjacket. Axel aimed his dart gun at the guy's chest and pulled the trigger. Nikki waited for the last Power Trapper to fall to the floor like the other two. But he didn't. Axel hadn't missed; rather, the gun didn't fire.

"Jammed," Axel said. He shook the gun and a dart clattered to the floor. The Power Trapper aimed his laser pistol at Axel's head. Nikki looked at the dart on the floor. She knew what she had to do. She rolled once, snatching the dart in her hand as she tumbled across the floor. In one motion she got to her feet and started running toward the Power Trapper. He swiveled his pistol at her and fired three laser bursts. The lasers were fast, but Nikki was faster. She juked once, juked twice, and ducked. Each of the lasers sailed past her harmlessly.

Whipping her hand forward, she threw the dart at the guy. It fluttered in the air for a moment and looked like it would fall short of him. But then, miraculously, the dart landed on his foot, piercing his shoe and sticking. His tongue wagged out and then he dropped like a rock.

Nikki turned and saw Axel grinning at her. "Three down," she said.

"Thanks," he said.

"Thanks to you, too," Nikki replied. "If your gun hadn't jammed, you would have beaten them all."

Mike and Freddy peeked around the corner. Freddy eyed the Power Trappers on the floor. "Are they…are they…dead?"

"No," Axel said. "Just sleeping. My gun only shoots tranquilizer darts. Perfect for putting big, dumb animals to sleep. Like these guys, for instance."

Nikki grinned at Axel. Maybe he wasn't so bad after all. "I guess that dart guns are better than laser pistols," she said.

15

Another power kid, no Samantha

Next to the sleeping Power Trappers, there was another gold door. *Surely this one will be Samantha*, Nikki thought. She tried one of the keys that she had gotten off the first guard. Too big again. The second key worked and the door clicked open. Because of her super-strength, Nikki didn't need Freddy and Mike to help her push the heavy door open this time. One touch of her finger and the door swung open. There was a girl cowering in the corner. She was sobbing into her hands. Definitely not Samantha. She had pale, freckled skin and a bright red shock of hair.

"Hi," Nikki said. She could feel Freddy's big head peeking over her shoulder.

The girl stopped crying and wiped her eyes with the back of her hand. She looked up at Nikki with tear-stained cheeks. Her eyes were wide and surprised, but filled with sadness, too. She had big, silver hoop earrings through a hole in each of her earlobes. "Who are you?" she asked.

"I'm Nikki Powergloves." Nikki didn't want to frighten her, so she approached slowly. "I have some friends outside. Mike Powerscarves, Freddy Powersocks, and, uh, Axel Powerjackets."

The girl's eyes widened even further. She stared at Nikki's gloves. "Do those give you the ability to…...*do things?*"

Nikki laughed. "If you mean, do I have powers, then yes. We all do." The girl's eyes slipped past Nikki. Nikki glanced back. The others were in the doorway. Except for Axel, who was leaning against the wall in the passage. He looked bored.

How is this possible?" the girl asked. "I thought I was the only one who had powers. I thought I was a freak."

Nikki laughed again. "Well, you might be a freak, but if so, we're all freaks, I guess."

The girl finally smiled. She looked pretty when she smiled. Nikki extended a hand. "What's your name?" Nikki asked.

The girl took her hand and Nikki easily pulled her to her feet. "Britney," she said. "Britney Mosely."

Nikki cocked her head to the side. It sounded weird for the girl to say her last name when Nikki knew she was a power kid. She was getting used to everyone's name being Joe or Jane Power*something*. "That's a pretty name," Nikki said. Britney's cheeks turned pink. "Where do you get your powers from?" Nikki asked.

Britney's hands automatically lifted to her ears and she started tugging at her earrings. "From these," she said.

"Then your superhero name will be Britney Powerearrings," Nikki said.

"Superhero? Me?"

"Of course, all the power kids are superheroes. Or super villains. Let me guess, you've got twelve different pairs of earrings," Nikki said.

"Right! How'd you know?"

"We all have twelve powers, too. We don't know everything about our powers, but we're starting to learn. We can tell you everything we know after we get you out of here. You can join our group if you like."

Britney's smile was back and bigger than ever. It was practically lighting up her face. "You really mean it? That would be great! It's been so lonely thinking I was the only freak. Not that you're a freak," she added quickly.

"Don't worry about it," Nikki said with a wave of her hand. "We're all a little odd. Wait until you meet Spencer."

"Who?"

"Never mind. First we need to find our other friend and get out of here. Have you seen another girl in here somewhere?"

Britney shook her head. "Sorry. I thought I was the only one. When you came in I thought the big men were going to hurt me."

"The Power Trappers," Nikki said. "That's what they call themselves. For some reason they're trying to round us all up. I think they want to experiment on us or something. Or try to take our powers. But don't worry. We look out for each other. From now on you'll be part of our team."

Britney clapped her hands. "Thanks!" she said. Her smile faded to a worried frown. "But how will we escape. There are so many of those big men."

"Don't worry about that, Britney. We've got more than a few tricks up our sleeves," Nikki said.

16

The third golden door

They followed Axel down the hall, away from Britney's cell. Tiny butterflies were swirling around in Nikki stomach. She was excited. They had rescued two new power kids *and* they were about to rescue Samantha. Their mission had gone perfectly. She couldn't wait to tell Spencer.

The hallway ended and Axel turned sharply to the left. Like before, he raised his dart gun and prepared to fire. Nikki watched pensively, waiting for the lasers to start flying over his head. Nothing. No lasers. No *Bizzzzz!* of Axel's dart gun. Just nothing.

Nikki rounded the corner and looked past Axel. The passage was empty and silent. She could see the shiny gold door on the right. There was no guard, no chair. *The third golden door*, Nikki thought. Samantha. Hopefully.

The rest of the power kids gathered around Nikki. "What do you make of it, Nikki?" Freddy asked.

Nikki shrugged. "Maybe the three guards outside Britney's door were the last of them."

"I wouldn't count on it," Axel said negatively.

Nikki ignored him and walked past, approaching the golden door silently. The butterflies fluttered faster. She tried the third key, the one that hadn't worked on either of the other two golden doors. The biggest key.

It fit perfectly and slid into the keyhole. She twisted her wrist, turning the key in the lock. It clicked. With one super-strength arm she pushed the heavy door open.

The girl was facing away from the door, but Nikki knew right away who it was. Her blond, curly locks and wide, brown belt gave her away.

"Samantha!" Nikki exclaimed.

Samantha turned, her eyes wide with surprise. "Nikki?" she said.

They ran forward and hugged each other. Nikki closed her eyes and felt the butterflies disappear. Everything was going to be fine. "We're here to rescue you," Nikki said.

With her hands still on Nikki's shoulders, Samantha pulled back from the hug so she could see Nikki's face. "Who's with you?"

Just as Samantha spoke, Mike and Freddy spilled into the room, big grins highlighting their faces. They joined in the group hug as the Power Council, minus the sidekicks, was rejoined. There was laughter and smiles for a few minutes until Nikki noticed Britney standing awkwardly to the side. She was looking at her feet.

"There's someone you need to meet," Nikki said to Samantha. Samantha looked at Nikki strangely. Nikki gestured for Samantha to turn around. "This is Britney Powerearrings," she said. "Britney—meet Samantha Powerbelts."

Somehow Samantha knew the right thing to say. "Were you a prisoner here, too?"

Britney looked up. She nodded.

Samantha extended her hand and smiled. "Not anymore," she said. "Now you're a member of the Power Council."

Britney's eyes lit up again, all awkwardness gone. She shook Samantha's hand vigorously. "Thank you, thank you so much!"

A heavily accented voice said from the hall, "Enough of this mushy stuff. We need to get out of here."

Samantha's head jerked to the side to see who had spoken. Nikki said, "There's one more person you need to meet, Samantha."

Before Nikki could say another word, Axel strode into the room and extended a hand. "Axel Powerjackets," he said. "Not looking for any new friends. Just want to get out of this place."

Samantha shook his hand quickly. She didn't reply. Nikki noticed that Samantha's eyes looked angry as she looked at Axel. Like she knew something about him. Nikki wondered what it might be.

Freddy said, "Axel's right. We need to go."

Axel glared at Freddy. "Thanks for your approval, butterball," he said sarcastically.

Freddy took a step forward, his hands clenched at his sides.

Nikki stepped between them for the second time that day and said, "This is not the time or the place to fight," she said. "Axel—keep your comments to yourself. Freddy—just try to ignore Axel."

Samantha's eyebrows rose and her lips curled into a grin. Nikki blushed. "Sorry, I just thought—" Nikki started to say.

Samantha cut her off: "It's okay, Nikki. It seems like you've been a great leader while I've been gone," she said.

Nikki's face reddened even further. "I'm glad you're back," was all she could think of to say.

"Me, too," Samantha said. "Now let's go!"

She charged out of the room. Axel followed quickly after her. Freddy and Mike squeezed through the door at the same time. When Nikki didn't move, Britney walked out next.

Nikki took a deep breath. She was happy to be at the back of the pack. Samantha was back, and she could retake her spot as the leader. Nikki clapped her gloves together and laughed loudly. Still laughing, she raced out the door. She heard the smack of ten sneakers running along the floor in front of her.

17

The Power Trappers final trap

After running along the hall, turning, running down another hall, and climbing about two dozen steps, Nikki caught up to her friends. They were waiting for her at the top of the staircase. There was a door at the top. Samantha had opened it a crack and was peeking through.

"It's really dark in there. I don't know where it leads," Samantha said.

Nikki squeezed past her friends, almost getting stuck when she slipped past Freddy's big belly. She stuck an eye to the crack. It was too dark to see, so she stuck a hand through. She felt soft cloth. Lots of it. Hanging from a rack. She grinned and pulled the door the whole way open.

"It's the closet in the cabin," she said. "We thought it was just a closet, but it's another secret way down here." Moving her hands like she was swimming, Nikki pushed the jackets and hanging clothes to each side, so she could see the closet door. Ever so slowly, she turned the knob on the closet door and pushed.

Light spilled into the closet. She didn't hear any voices. Didn't see any big Power Trappers. The cabin appeared to be empty, just like they left it. "Clear," Nikki said.

They marched into the cabin. "Where are we?" Samantha said. "They had a bag over my head when they brought me here."

"A cabin in the woods," Nikki said. "Outside of Cragglyville."

"Where are the Power Trappers?" Samantha said.

"Let's just say that a bunch of them stepped in something sticky," Nikki said.

"Yeah, and three others got really sleepy," Axel said.

Nikki opened the front door to show Samantha what she meant. Nikki gasped.

The big men were gone, and in their place were three kids. One was a small boy wearing dark sunglasses. He grinned a toothy grin at her. "Sorry, Nikki," Spencer said. He was stuck in the glue! The other two kids were Chilly and Dexter and they were stuck, too!

Before Nikki could even begin to think about how Spencer had ended up stuck in his own glue, or how the Power Trappers had gotten loose, a huge *BOOM!* shook the cabin. A monstrous ball of steel tore through the roof, spewing chunks of wood and plaster from above. Nikki ducked and felt the gritty rain collapse on her head. When she uncovered her face, the air was thick with a dusty haze. She looked up and saw a wide hole in the roof with blue sky above it.

BOOM! Another ear-shattering blast sounded and more debris collapsed from above. Someone grabbed Nikki's arm, and she heard Samantha say, "Out, out, out!"

Nikki and her friends became a mob as they pushed through the front door. Then she remembered what lay in front of them. But it was too late. *Squish, squish!* She took two steps and knew they were done for. When she tried to lift her legs, they held firmly to the ground. They had been stuck by Spencer's Sticky Situation Glue.

"Oops," Spencer said. "We in biiiiiiiiiiig trouble!" he yelled.

"What is this stuff?" Axel demanded. He was pulling at his leg, trying to get it unstuck.

"Don't worry about that now, we have to figure out a way to escape!" Samantha exclaimed.

"There is no escape," a man said. The power kids twisted and turned toward the voice.

"Oh no," Nikki said under her breath. The man was her dad, and he was walking toward them. On either side of him were the Power Trappers, looking mean and angry. They were carrying nets. Behind them was a huge black machine with big metal treads like an army tank. A bulky man was driving it. From the front, a steel arm extended high into the air. A big, metal wrecking ball hung from the arm.

Her dad said, "Looking for something?" He gently tossed a canister back and forth from his left hand to his right hand and back again.

"I'm sorry, Willy-Nilly," Spencer said. "They caught me and made me give them the antidote spray for the Sticky Situation Glue."

"It's not your fault," Nikki said, deepening her voice to try to disguise it from her dad. Thankfully, she was wearing her superhero disguise, with her braid across her eyes.

Mr. Nickerson took another step forward. "Anyone got any ideas?" Samantha said.

Instead of answering, Axel whipped out his dart gun and fired. The dart hit one of the Power Trappers, who slumped to the ground and started snoring. One of the other Power Trappers immediately pulled out his laser gun and let loose a green burst of light.

Axel was stuck to the ground. Just like the rest of them. He couldn't move. Couldn't dodge the laser. The light beam connected with his dart gun and knocked it out of his hand. The gun clattered against the cabin, out of reach.

"Anyone have a better idea?" Samantha said, glaring at Axel.

Freddy suddenly pumped a chubby fist in the air and said, "Yeah! I've got it!" He paused for a moment and then yelled, "Anti-gravity!"

Something weird happened. Nikki's dad, the Power Trappers, the cars parked nearby, and even the monstrous wrecking truck, all started to float up into the air. Nikki remembered watching a show about astronauts on TV with Spencer. It looked like that. Like they were in outer space, on the moon. Like gravity didn't exist anymore. Except that Nikki and her friends were still safely on the ground. Because they were stuck with the glue.

Freddy's gray sock, Nikki remembered. She didn't know what power it would give him when he first put it on, but now she knew it was anti-gravity! "Brilliant idea, Freddy!" she exclaimed. Freddy beamed at the compliment.

"Yeah, but now what?" Axel said. "We're still stuck."

"I think I can help with that," Nikki said. It was time to put her super-strength to the ultimate test. It was her strength against Spencer's incredibly sticky glue. Using all her strength she lifted her leg. She felt her muscles tighten, straining against the glue's firm hold on her sneakers. Her veins were bulging in her leg.

At first nothing happened.

But then she felt something give. Not the glue—it was way too strong, even for Nikki—but the earth beneath the glue. With a *Crack!* Nikki's foot lifted off the ground, carrying a clump of dirt with it. She was so strong that she barely noticed the extra weight.

She strained her other leg. *Crack!* It broke free, too, leaving her mobile once again. She started to float upwards, as the effect of the anti-gravity hit her.

Spencer yelled, "Goooo, Boss-Lady!"

"Freddy—anti-gravity off, now!" Nikki yelled.

Freddy snapped his fingers and Nikki dropped solidly to the ground. Her dad and the Power Trappers were higher than her, and they fell too, landing awkwardly, tumbling to the earth and scattering in all directions. The parked cars crashed down, making loud screeching and scraping sounds. Their fenders were dented and some of their tires were flattened. The gigantic wrecking truck was the last to land, hitting the ground with a deafening *BOOOOOM!* The steel wrecking ball landed on top of the cabin, caving in what was left of the roof. All in all, when Freddy turned off the anti-gravity it was a more spectacular sight than when he had turned it on!

But Nikki wasn't paying attention to any of that. Her eyes were focused on the canister in her dad's hand. When he fell to the ground he did a somersault and lost his grip on the spray can. It rolled to a stop in the grass. Nikki moved so fast she was just a blur. She grabbed the can and raced back to her friends. With a loud *Shhhhhhh!* she sprayed what was left in the can all around her friends' feet. One by one, they pulled free.

The last kid she released was Spencer. He was grinning at her, his braces gleaming in the sunlight. "I knew you would rescue me!" he said.

Nikki grinned back. "We're not out of the woods yet," Nikki said.

Spencer looked at the trees that surrounded the clearing and laughed. "Good one, Comedy-Hour!"

Then the lasers started flying. Bright beams of blue and red and yellow burst all around them. Nikki saw a flash of light as a laser flew between her and Spencer. "Take cover!" she yelled. The six power kids and three sidekicks ran behind the parked cars. The lasers ricocheted off the glass windows and metal doors.

"What now?" Mike asked.

Samantha said, "Time for the brown belt." Nikki thought hard but couldn't remember what power the brown belt gave Samantha. That's when the cars came alive.

Suddenly they were moving all on their own, some rolling like normal, and others walking on their tires like feet. One was even bouncing like a rabbit. They were still blocking the lasers, but were moving closer to the Power Trappers.

"You get their guns, I'll take care of the nets!" Mike said, grabbing Nikki by the arm. "We're the fastest ones here."

In a twirl of arms and legs, Mike turned into a tornado and swirled ahead of Nikki, chasing after the animated cars. Nikki raced after him, quickly catching up and passing him. She shot past the moving cars and into the pack of Power Trappers. Nikki zigzagged through them, grabbing armfuls of laser guns as she passed each of them. She burst into the open and dropped the guns in a pile on the ground.

Behind her, the Power Trappers were getting spun and knocked around by the force of Mike the tornado. When he was finished, each and every Power Trapper was in a tangle of ropes and nets. Their arms stuck out through the holes in the netting like pins from a pin cushion. They looked silly. Nikki laughed.

She approached the bundle of big, strong, silly-looking men. Her dad was in the midst of them, just as tangled as they were. She felt a little bad about it, because he was her dad, but knew it was for the best. Making her voice sound deep, she said, "I hope you guys learned your lesson. Stay away from us. We are just trying to help people. We are the good guys, try to remember that."

Nikki's dad just stared at her. Nikki turned away from him and walked back to her friends. She had to hope that her dad would listen to what she said. When she saw Spencer, he gave her a big thumbs up and she couldn't help but smile. He smiled, too, but then his smile faded and he started to run toward her. "Look out!" he yelled.

Nikki whirled around just in time to see a Power Trapper sitting high on the wrecking truck. They had all forgotten about the truck driver. His laser gun was aimed right at Nikki. The laser had already left the gun. All Nikki could see was the red beam of light. No matter how quick she was she wouldn't be able to get out of the way. The red changed to green, not because the laser changed color, but because something big and green jumped in front of Nikki. The red beam of light reflected off of Freddy's turtle shell and collided harmlessly with the dirt.

Bizzzzz! The dart flew through the air, its feathered tail swirling behind it. *Thwop!* It hit the Power Trapper in the shoulder and he

112

slumped to the side. He was asleep. Nikki spun around and saw Axel holding his dart gun in the air.

He lowered his weapon and said, "That's for saving my life earlier."

"Now we're even," Nikki said.

Samantha seemed to be watching the exchange with Nikki with interest. Her eyes skipped back and forth between Axel and Nikki. She said, "Thanks, Axel."

"Whatever," Axel said.

Nikki said, "Do you want to join the Power Council, Axel?"

He said, "No thanks."

Samantha frowned and said, "Are you going to join the Power Outlaws?"

"I'm not joining anyone," Axel said. "See you all later." He opened his powerchest and took off his denim jacket. He dropped it in the chest and pulled out a blue windbreaker with a picture of an eagle on the front. He put one arm in a sleeve and then the other. Zipped it up. Beautiful white eagle wings burst from his back and beat strongly behind him. With a *whooosh!* of air, he took off, flying higher and higher until he was just a speck in the sky.

Nikki watched him go and then said, "Will we ever see him again?"

Samantha said, "I can almost guarantee we will."

Spencer said, "Let's go home, whoop, whoop!"

Nikki liked that idea. She was ready to go home, for a while at least. They had defeated the Power Trappers and could go back to being kid superheroes.

Each of the remaining power kids switched their powers into one that was good for travelling, and left the entangled Power Trappers behind them. They were headed for home.

18

Home sweet home

Nikki was at home, sitting at the dinner table talking to her parents. Life seemed to be back to normal. She had flown to Spencer's house, dropped him off, and then walked home. Her mom had made dinner. Her dad had come home from work. He had a scratch on his forehead and his arms and legs were red and swollen. He told Nikki and her mom that he fell down at work, but was just fine.

Nikki had smiled. Said, "That's good, Dad. I'm glad you're okay." She had given him a big hug. He didn't seem as angry anymore. No more frowns. Just big smiles. Perhaps he *had* learned his lesson. She didn't really think he was a bad guy. He was probably just scared of what the power kids could do. She hoped he wouldn't work with the Power Trappers anymore.

At dinner they talked like a normal family. About normal family things. About the new trick Mr. Miyagi had learned at doggie school, about the weather, about what they were going to watch on TV that night. Nikki enjoyed it. Somehow she knew it wouldn't last very long. Because she wasn't normal. She was Nikki Powergloves. A superhero!

She fell asleep that night and dreamed of Weebles and flying and golden doors and big black helicopters. When she woke up the next morning she could still see flashes of light from the lasers in her dreams. She blinked a few times and the lasers disappeared.

She lay in bed for a minute. Soft breathing sighed up from below her. *Mr. Miyagi.* She listened to his breathing for a while, just enjoying how normal it sounded. It was good to be home. *Home sweet home*, she thought.

She heard a buzz on her nightstand as her cell phone rattled on the wood. It was a text message from Samantha. She read what it had to say:

BIG News! Come to the Power City. Bring Spencer.

Nikki smiled. Her normal summer day was over already. But she didn't mind. She loved the adventure in her life. After getting dressed, she jogged over to Spencer's house, showed him the message, and took off toward the Power City with her friend on her back.

During the entire trip Spencer talked about how cool the fight against the Power Trappers had been. He said, "Like when Samantha brought the cars to life, remember? It was like *Transformers!*"

Nikki just listened, enjoying Spencer's excitement. It was still early so the wind felt cool on her skin. The sun was slowly warming the air as it climbed above a low bank of clouds.

Soon the mountain rose in the distance. Nikki started to head for the peak, where the secret entrance to the Power City was located, but then saw a commotion at the base of the mountain. A bunch of tiny dots were moving around. She headed for them.

As they approached, the dots began to take shape. Gnomes, and Weebles, and power kids, and sidekicks. All dancing and singing and having a good time. Waiting for Nikki and Spencer. Even Britney was there, smiling and dancing. Like she was already part of the team.

Nikki landed softly and Spencer slid off of her back. They joined in the festivities, moving through the throng of happy people and creatures. She spotted Chuck the gnome and made her way over to him. "Hi, Chuck!" she said.

"Princess Nikki. What a pleasure it is to see you again," he said with a small bow.

"You, too, Chuck. And thanks again for all your help yesterday. We couldn't have done it without the help of the gnomes."

He bowed again, and said, "You can count us as your friends. Call on us whenever you need us." Then he shook his butt and danced into a crowd of other gnomes.

Nikki laughed and looked for the other power kids. Samantha was nearby, dancing with a familiar Weeble. "Roy!" Nikki exclaimed.

The small, black Weeble looked even smaller without his big, poofy wedding dress on. "Hey, Nikki!" he said. Samantha was spinning him around with one hand.

Samantha said, "Thanks for coming, Nikki."

"Of course," Nikki said. "Is this a party to celebrate defeating the Power Trappers?"

"Why don't you ask Roy," Samantha said.

Nikki cocked her head to the side in puzzlement. Why wouldn't Samantha just tell her?

"Roy?" Nikki said.

"What?" Roy said.

"What's the party for?" Nikki asked.

Roy looked at her like she was crazy. He said, "Because today we are getting a message from the Power Giver!"

19

A message from the Power Giver

After they finished dancing and singing, the odd group of Weebles, gnomes, power kids, and sidekicks entered the mountain and made their way to Weebleville. Samantha explained everything to Nikki and Spencer as they walked along.

Early that morning, the Great Weeble had summoned Roy to Weeble Tower. He told him that he had received a message from the Power Giver. *The message was for the power kids*, he told Roy. Roy immediately contacted Samantha, who contacted the power kids and their sidekicks. Roy also couldn't help but to tell the gnomes, because he was friends with them. So now they were all gathering in Weebleville to hear the message from the Power Giver.

They were in the fire tunnel—almost to Weebleville. Nikki tried to remember what the Great Weeble had told them about the Power Giver. Not much. As if reading her mind, Spencer said, "I think all we know about this Power Giver dude is that he is the one who gave all the power kids their powers, cheep cheep!"

Nikki nodded. That sounded right. But who was he? And why did he choose her to give the powergloves to? Why couldn't they meet him?

Her questions would have to wait, however, because they had reached Weebleville. Everyone poured inside. The Weebles were rolling, the gnomes were jogging to keep up, and the kids were walking. A big stage had been built. Probably by Mike.

Everyone sat in front of the stage. Nikki was next to Spencer and Britney. Britney's eyes were wide and excited. It was her first time in the Power City and she seemed to be enjoying it very much. The rest of her friends were sitting around her. There was Samantha and Roy in front of her, Chilly, Dexter, and Freddy to the left, and Mike and Chuck the gnome to the right. Everyone was chattering in excitement.

Nikki was listening to her friends' guess what the Great Weeble would say, when a sudden hush fell over the crowd. The tiny Weeble they had met in the tippy-top of Weeble Tower rolled onto the stage. He looked even smaller in front of such a big crowd.

He cleared his throat. "Hi, y'all!" the Great Weeble said. There was a mixture of clapping, cheers, whistles, and catcalls throughout the crowd. He waited for the noise to finish. "I'm bettin' my boots you ain't here to watch me do a tap dance," he said. There was a mixture of laughter and groans. He continued: "Now, now, don't worry your little flea-brains about it. I won't be dancin' or singin'. I'm sure y'all heard the news. I've got a message fer these here power kids." He motioned to Nikki and her group of friends. Every head in the crowd turned to stare at them. Nikki played with her hands until the heads turned back toward the stage.

"The message is from the Power Giver!" the Great Weeble said grandly. The cheers grew louder and louder. The Weebles were the loudest of all. They seemed to love the Power Giver, or at least the idea of the Power Giver. She wondered if any of them had even met him. He seemed so mysterious to her.

The Great Weeble continued: "The Power Giver asked me to tell y'all that he is holdin' a quest fer all the power kids and their sidekicks." A hush once more fell over the crowd. "It will be called….The Great Adventure!"

Nikki and Spencer looked at each other and grinned. With just their smiles, they said more words to each other than if they had been talking for ten minutes. They said that they were best friends; that they would be there for each other; and that they were about to go on the greatest adventure of their lives.

And they would do it together.

THE END (of this Adventure!)

Keep reading for a peek into David Estes's magical fourth book in the Nikki Powergloves adventure, *Nikki Powergloves and the Great Adventure.*

Hero Card

Hidden Identity: Nikki Powergloves
Birth Name: Nikki Nickerson
Age: 9
Height: 4 feet, 2 inches
Weight: 67 pounds
Sidekick: Spencer Quick, certified genius
Known Allies: Samantha Powerbelts, Freddy Powersocks, Michael Powerscarves, Britney Powerearrings
Source of Power: Gloves

Powers

Glove Color	Glove Picture	Power
White	Snowflake	Create ice
Red	Flame	Create fire
Light blue	Bird	Fly
Black & yellow	Lightning Bolt	Control the weather
Green	Leaf	Super-grow plants
Purple	Muscly arm	Super-strength
Orange	Shoes	Super-speed
Gray	No picture	Invisibility
Brown	Paw print	Transform into an animal
Pink	Tarot card	See the future
Gold	Clock	Freeze or slow down time
Peach	Two identical stick figures	Transform into someone else

Hero Card

Hidden Identity: Samantha Powerbelts
Birth Name: Samantha Jane McKinley
Age: 9
Height: 4 feet, 6 inches
Weight: 77 pounds
Sidekick: Dexter Chan, excellent booby trapper
Known Allies: Nikki Powergloves, Freddy Powersocks, Michael Powerscarves, Britney Powerearrings
Source of Power: Belts

Powers

Belt Color	Belt Picture	Power
Brown	Dancing teddy bear	Make objects come to life
Peach	Six-armed girl	Grow extra arms/legs
Multi-colored	Paintbrush	Change objects' color
Silver	Shield	Dome of protection
Gold	Key	Open any door/lock
Bright red	Smile	Make people laugh
White	Gum	Shoot sticky stuff
Blue	Snorkel	Breathe underwater
Orange	Rope	Shoot ropes from hands
Clear	Diamonds	Turn rocks to jewels
Green	Walking trees	Make trees come alive
Yellow	Spider	Climb walls like a spider

Hero Card

Hidden Identity: Freddy Powersocks
Birth Name: Frederick Nixon
Age: 9
Height: 4 feet, 5 inches
Weight: 95 pounds
Sidekick: Chilly Weathers, amateur magician
Known Allies: Nikki Powergloves, Samantha Powerbelts, Michael Powerscarves, Britney Powerearrings
Source of Power: Socks

Powers

Sock Color	Sock Picture	Power
White with black polka dots	Dog barking at a boy	Ability to speak to animals
Gray	Astronaut	Anti-gravity
Camouflage	Chameleon	Camouflage himself
Gold	Wristwatch	Change rate of time
Black	Nunchucks	Ninja skills
Peach	Girl slapping a boy	Distance slap
Pink	Brain	Read people's thoughts
Brown	Shovel	Dig huge tunnels
Black & Yellow	Bumblebee	Turn into a bumblebee
Purple	Microphone	Impersonate voices
Green	Turtle shell	Grow a shell
Fuzzy brown	Monkey	Control a horde of monkeys

Hero Card

Hidden Identity: Mike Powerscarves
Birth Name: Michael Jones
Age: 9
Height: 4 feet, 2 inches
Weight: 67 pounds
Sidekick: None
Known Allies: Nikki Powergloves, Samantha Powerbelts, Freddy Powersocks, Britney Powerearrings
Source of Power: Scarves

Powers

Scarf Color	Scarf Picture	Power
Black	Car tire	Turn body to rubber
Blue & Gold striped	Tall pole	Leap high in the air
Gray	Hammer	Ability to build anything
Green	Ice cream cone	Create food
Brown striped	Tornado	Spin tornado-fast
Red & Yellow polka dots	10 stick figures	Break into 10 mini-Mikes
Black & white	Magnifying glass	Disappear sideways
All colors checkered	Plus sign	Boost other kids' powers
White	Steering wheel	Drive any vehicle
Brown & black checkered	Minus sign	Decrease other kids' powers
Orange	Hovercraft	Ride a hovercraft
Green & red polka dots	Dinosaur tail	Grow dinosaur tail

Hero Card

Hidden Identity: Britney Powerearrings
Birth Name: Britney Mosely
Age: 9
Height: 4 feet, 2 inches
Weight: 63 pounds
Sidekick: None
Known Allies: Nikki Powergloves, Samantha Powerbelts, Freddy Powersocks, Mike Powerscarves
Source of Power: Earrings

Powers

Earring Color	Earring Shape	Power
Silver	Large hoops	Super discs
Red	Hearts	Love potion
Blue	Butterflies	Change into butterfly
Clear	Diamonds	Become as hard as diamonds
Gold	Small hoops	Mini discs
Black	Long dangly	Pixie sticks
Green	Leaves	Leaf monster
Pink	Flowers	Soft flower bed
Brown	Feathers	Pointy feather attack
White	Angel wings	Grow angel wings
Silver with turquoise stone	Square with inlaid gem	Create big stone blocks
Red ruby	Gemstones	Red laser beams

Loner Card

Hidden Identity: Axel Powerjackets
Birth Name: Axel Grant
Age: 9
Height: 4 feet, 8 inches
Weight: 75 pounds
Sidekick: None
Known Allies: None
Source of Power: Jackets

Powers

Jacket Color	Jacket Picture	Power
Blue denim	Feathered darts	Dart gun
Black leather	Ghost	Ghost attack
Beige cloth	Cow	Cow stampede
Blue windbreaker	Eagle	Sprout wings
Heavy gray wool	Slinky	Slinky movement
Blue & red flannel	Ape wearing a crown	Turn into King Kong
Red nylon	Rocket	Turn into a missile
Green pullover	Elf	Elf mischief
White sweatshirt	Ski poles	Super skier
Dark orange fleece	Orange fruit	Become a giant orange
Brown tattered zip-up	Boot	Big boot
Yellow stylish	Ferrari	Yellow Ferrari driver

Villain Card

Hidden Identity: Jimmy Powerboots (previously known as Jimmy- Boy Wonder)
Birth Name: Timothy Jonathan Sykes (nicknamed Jimmy)
Age: 9
Height: 4 feet, 1 inch
Weight: 65 pounds
Sidekick: unknown
Known Allies: Peter Powerhats, Naomi Powerskirts
Source of Power: Boots

Powers

Boot Color	Boot Picture	Power
Black	Cracked ground	Powerstomp
Purple	One leg on each side of a wall	Walk through walls
Orange	Floating bananas	Move objects with mind
Red	Boots with flame	Rocket boots
White	5 identical stick figures	Clone himself
Yellow	Half-boy here, half-boy there	Teleport
Blue	Wall of water	Control water
Brown	Big ear	Super senses
Green	Computer	Computer hacking
Red/blue/yellow	Wires	Skills with electronics
Gray	Yellow pages	Find anyone in the world
Gold & black checkered	Clock	Speed up time

Villain Card

Hidden Identity: Peter Powerhats
Birth Name: Peter Hurley
Age: 9
Height: 4 feet, 10 inch
Weight: 100 pounds
Sidekick: unknown
Known Allies: Jimmy Powerboots, Naomi Powerskirts
Source of Power: Hats

Powers

Hat Color	Hat Picture	Power
Bright gold	Powerchest	Find lost powerchests
Neon green	Strong man	Grow big and strong
Black	Cannonball	Turn into cannonball
Gray	Stones	Makes stones form
Red	Bull horns	Transform into a raging bull
Peach	Big hand	Grow big hands
Blue	Big wheels	Drive a monster truck
Orange	Mouth and fire	Burp fireballs
Green	Fingers holding nost	Stinky farts
Purple	Strawberry jelly	Turn body to jelly
Brown	Porcupine	Cover body in prickly spines
Clear	Teardrops	Make people cry

Villain Card

Hidden Identity: Naomi Powerskirts
Birth Name: Naomi Lee
Age: 9
Height: 4 feet, 0 inches
Weight: 55 pounds
Sidekick: unknown
Known Allies: Jimmy Powerboots, Peter Powerhats
Source of Power: Skirts

Powers

Skirt Color	Skirt Picture	Power
Yellow	Sun	Travel on light beams
Green	Ogre	Turn into an ugly monster
Blue	Three skirts	Change powers fast
Black	Light bulb	Control electricity
Brown	Mud	Create gobs of mud
Pink	Gymnast	Gymnastics skills
Purple	Mirror	Mix up the world
Gray	Foot on water	Walk on anything
Orange	Closed eye	Laser winks
Pink & black striped	Skateboard	Skateboarding skills
Black with green polka dots	Plant with arms	Grow fighting plants
Turquoise	Pigeon	Attack pigeons

Acknowledgements

To those kids who have made it through the third *Nikki Powergloves* adventure, I thank you for sticking with Nikki and Spencer! There are more adventures ahead and they're all for you!

Thanks to my wife, my family, my friends, and my Goodreads fan club, for your unending support and word-of-mouth marketing. You are my superheroes.

Thanks to Nicole Passante and Karla Calzada at shareAread. You are true book-promoting-marketing ninjas!

Thank you again to my all-star team of kid beta readers and their moms. You gave this series a chance to be something special. So thank you to D'vora Gelfond and her niece Maia Farina, Adriana Noriega and her son Jordan, Brooke Del Vecchio and her son Anthony, and Gabriela Racine and her son Carlos.

Finally, the biggest thanks ever to my cover artists/designers at Winkipop Designs, who made the third *Nikki Powergloves* cover even better than the first two!

Discover other books by David Estes available through the author's official website:

http://davidestes100.blogspot.com or through select online retailers including Amazon.

Children's Books by David Estes

The Nikki Powergloves Adventures:
Nikki Powergloves- A Hero is Born
Nikki Powergloves and the Power Council
Nikki Powergloves and the Power Trappers
Nikki Powergloves and the Great Adventure
Nikki Powergloves vs. the Power Outlaws (coming in 2013!)

Young-Adult Books by David Estes

The Dwellers Saga:
Book One—The Moon Dwellers
Book Two—The Star Dwellers (Coming September 30 2012!)

The Evolution Trilogy:
Book One—Angel Evolution
Book Two—Demon Evolution
Book Three—Archangel Evolution

Connect with David Estes Online

Facebook:
http://www.facebook.com/pages/David-Estes/130852990343920

Author's blog:
http://davidestesbooks.blogspot.com

Smashwords:
http://www.smashwords.com/profile/view/davidestes100

Goodreads author page: http://www.goodreads.com/davidestesbooks

Twitter:
https://twitter.com/#!/davidestesbooks

About the Author

After growing up in Pittsburgh, Pennsylvania, David Estes moved to Sydney, Australia, where he met his wife, Adele. Now they travel the world writing and reading and taking photographs.

1

Spencer goes skydiving without a parachute

Her wings sparkled under the rays of the noonday sun. The fluffy, white wings looked like they were covered in diamonds, shimmering and glittering. They matched her beautiful diamond earrings. But she didn't know how to use her wings properly. Nikki was trying to teach her.

"Turn, Britney, turn!" Nikki shouted. Nikki was hovering magically in the air. She was wearing her blue flying powergloves. The ones with the picture of the bird on them.

Slowly, Britney banked to the left, completing a huge circle and coming around to face Nikki. Nikki grimaced. Britney was going to need a lot more training. But now she needed encouragement.

"Good job, Britney. That was a lot better than last time," Nikki said. "Let me show you again."

Britney smiled her dazzling smile. "Thanks, Nikki." When Nikki and her friends had first rescued Britney from the lair of the Power Trappers—the evil men who were trying to capture the power kids—Britney wore one of the saddest expressions that Nikki had ever seen. Now, her face was the complete opposite, filled with joy and happiness. Nikki couldn't help but to smile back.

"Okay, watch closely," Nikki said. She took off like a rocket, bursting through the thin air with a power and speed usually reserved for airplanes and missiles. She was at home in the air, as if she was born to fly. She loved everything about it. The feeling of the wind whipping through her hair, the exhilaration of a sharp drop toward the ground, the feeling of control over her body as she zigzagged across the sky.

Relying on instinct only, Nikki cut sharply to the left, and then to the left again, carving a V in the sky with her path. In less than a second, she had turned and was heading back in the opposite direction, toward Britney. Then, as if using her feet to skid across the air, Nikki slid to a stop next to her new friend.

"That's how it's done," Nikki said.

Britney clapped her hands in excitement. Her hair looked even redder under the brightness of the sun and next to her sparkling white wings. Nikki noticed that Britney's face had even more freckles now than when she first met her. It was probably a result of all the time they had spent training outside. It was summer and most days were sunny.

"That was incredible, Nikki!" Britney exclaimed. "I don't think I'll ever be able to fly like you."

Nikki grinned. "You are doing great. All it takes is practice."

Nikki was about to teach Britney how to perform a midair somersault, when she heard a loud "Whoop whoop!" from behind her. Her smile got even bigger as she spun around.

"Spencer!" she yelled.

The silver hovercraft sliced through the air effortlessly. At first Nikki couldn't see Spencer, because Mike's body was blocking him. Mike was riding the hovercraft like a surfboard, his arms out to the side to keep his balance. His bright orange powerscarf was fluttering on the breeze. Like Nikki's blue gloves gave her the power to fly, Mike's orange scarf created his magical hovercraft.

A face with a toothy grin peeked around Mike. "Whoop whoop!" he yelled again. And then, "Incoming!"

Mike zoomed past Nikki and Britney, and Spencer leapt from the hovercraft, apparently trying to grab onto Nikki. However, his little legs weren't strong enough and he fell short, flailing his arms and legs wildly in the air as he tried to grab onto something that wasn't there.

"Augh!" he yelped.

He plummeted toward the ground.

Nikki grinned at Britney and said, "Duty calls," and then dove for the earth below her. She immediately locked her flight path on Spencer's falling body. Using all her energy, she pushed her body to its limits as she sped up, catching up to him in mere seconds. Once she was alongside him, she glanced to the side and made eye contact with her friend. His eyes were wide with fear and his mouth was open wide as if he was screaming, but he wasn't making any sound.

Above the roar of the wind, Nikki said, "Nice day for a fall, don't you think?"

Spencer's eyes widened further and his mouth closed and then opened again. He did this several times, like a fish out of water gasping for air, but couldn't seem to be able to make a sound. He looked down. Nikki glanced down, too, and saw that the ground was getting bigger and bigger, as if it was rising up to meet them halfway.

Nikki twisted her body so she was directly beneath her friend and then gently slowed her fall. She felt Spencer's legs lock onto her back and wrap around her. Once she knew he was securely on her back, Nikki leveled out and then shot into the air, like a space shuttle launching. In seconds she was as high as Britney, who had watched the entire event in awe.

"That was an amazing rescue, Nikki!" she said.

Mike raced over on his hovercraft. "Nikki, I'm so sorry, I didn't know—"

"It's okay, Mike, you couldn't have known Spencer was going to go skydiving without a parachute." Nikki glanced back at Spencer. "What do you have to say for yourself?"

"That was incredible! Whizzzz! I was so scared I thought I was going to wet my pants. It was the single most funny/scary thing I have ever done!" Spencer exclaimed.

Nikki sighed. "Spencer, sometimes I think you have cotton for brains," she said.

"I'm a genius, remember, Miracle-Flyer? It says so on my shirt," Spencer replied.

Spencer was wearing a black t-shirt that said "Certified Genius" across the front. Nikki knew that technically Spencer was a genius—at least that's what all the tests at school said—but sometimes…

"Genius or no genius, Spencer, you have no common sense sometimes. If I wasn't a superhero you might've died," Nikki blurted out.

"Well, if you weren't a superhero I never would have been way up in the air without a parachute," Spencer replied.

Nikki sighed again. Why was her best friend so good at arguing with her? She knew he was right. If she wasn't a superhero, both their lives would be much less dangerous.

"Okay, you two, no more arguing," Britney said smiling. "Spencer, you should be more careful next time, and Nikki, that was a fine rescue."

Nikki was mesmerized by Britney's smile. It seemed capable of making her feel better just by her seeing it. She immediately felt calmer.

"Let's go get some lunch, I am so hungry I could eat a pod of man-eating killer whales," Spencer said.

Everyone agreed and they played follow-the-leader back to the gray mountain in the distance. Mike led on his hovercraft and Nikki was able to stick close behind him while he did flips, sharp turns, and spins to try to shake them from his tail. Spencer screamed like a girl the whole time which made Nikki go even faster. Britney had a bit more trouble following the seasoned flyers, and quickly fell behind. When they reached the peak of the mountain, they waited for Britney to catch up.

When Spencer hopped off her back, Nikki glared at him. He just grinned at her and then stuck a finger up his nose and wiggled another finger from his ear, as if the finger up his nose had gone all the way through his brain and out his ear. Nikki tried to keep frowning at him—she was supposed to be angry at him, after all!—but wasn't able to stop herself from bursting out in laughter.

Spencer removed his finger from his nose and started laughing, too. He put an arm around her shoulder and said, "Fly-Girl, you can never stay mad at me, so I don't know why you even try."

Nikki ignored him and squirmed away and then lay on her back so she could look up at the clouds. They were on Phantom's Peak, aptly named for the ghostly gray clouds swirling above her. Sometimes Samantha Powerbelts—another one of Nikki's superhero friends—would use one of her powers to paint the clouds different colors. But now the clouds were just gray.

Finally, Britney caught up to them and landed awkwardly on the peak. Her feet got tangled together and although her wings flapped rapidly to try to keep her from falling, she tumbled over and landed face first. "Oomf!" she exclaimed.

Nikki tried to stifle her laughter as Mike helped Britney to her feet. Nikki said, "Tomorrow we'll have to practice landing."

Britney gave her a wry smile and nodded.

"Is it time to go down the slide?" Spencer asked excitedly.

In response to Spencer's question, Mike strode to the center of the peak and spoke directly into a round, metal hatch. "Mike, Nikki, Britney, and Spencer—back for lunch," he said.

The hatch popped open and a girl's voice said, "You may enter." It was Samantha's voice and Nikki loved hearing it. Just a few days earlier

Samantha, like Britney, had been imprisoned in one of the Power Trappers' gold cells, unable to use any of her powers. But now she was back, and had reclaimed her role as the unofficial leader of the Power Council.

When the hatch opened, Spencer ran for it yelling, "Cannonball!" and then leapt into the air, tucking his legs underneath him. He landed in the hole and they heard him scream, "Wickety wicket woo woo!" as he slid into the darkness.

Nikki, Mike, and Britney all laughed as their zany friend's voice echoed into the distance. Nikki let Mike and Britney go next, and then she followed them, plunging into the darkness feet first. The metal tube was slippery and she began to gain speed immediately, as she curved and dropped down the super-long slide that led deep into the mountain. Nikki got more and more excited as she continued to slide, because she knew what was at the bottom. *The Power City!* she thought.

Ever since Nikki had met Samantha, Mike, and Freddy Powersocks (yep, you guessed it, another kid with superpowers), she had loved going to the Power City with them. The underground network of caves and tunnels was the headquarters for the Power Council, of which Nikki was a member. Britney Powerearrings was the newest member and had brought their membership to eight kids, including the three sidekicks. Their main goal was to fight any bad kids who tried to use their superpowers for evil. So far, they had defeated a group of kids that called themselves the Power Outlaws from destroying Nikki's hometown of Cragglyville.

Nikki reached the end of the slide and dropped through the air. Instead of waiting to land on the soft mattress below her, she used her flying gloves to soar across the room and through the next door, which led into the Power City. Her friends were already through the door and making their way toward one of the many tunnels cut into the wall.

Samantha emerged from the tunnel to meet them.

"You're just in time. Roy has called a meeting about The Great Adventure and all power kids are invited to attend," Samantha said.

2

The last three power kids

Simultaneously, Nikki and Spencer looked at each other and said, "*All power kids?*"

Samantha nodded, her blond, curly locks of hair bobbing up and down with her head.

"You mean, like the bad guys, too?"

"I'm afraid so, Nikki," Samantha said.

Nikki's heart sank. All her elation from the ride down the slide vanished in a split second. Ideally, Nikki hoped to never have to see the Power Outlaws again, although she knew it was inevitable. But not this soon! And she certainly had hoped that the Power Outlaws would be excluded from The Great Adventure.

After Nikki and her friends had defeated the Power Trappers and rescued Samantha and Britney, the Great Weeble—the leader of the furry, half-porcupine, half-beaver creatures that lived in the Power City—announced that The Great Adventure would be held for all the power kids. Nikki assumed it would only be for the good power kids. Evidently she was wrong.

But why would the mysterious Power Giver want the super villains to participate in The Great Adventure? *The Power Giver*, Nikki thought. She knew almost nothing about him. Only that all the kids' powers were gifts from him. And that he was hosting The Great Adventure, whatever that was. Nikki was looking forward to finding out more about The Great Adventure, but was NOT looking forward to seeing the Power Outlaws—especially her arch nemesis, Jimmy Powerboots.

While she was thinking about how much she disliked the Power Outlaws, Spencer was thinking about something else. "Will Axel Powerjackets be there?" he asked.

"If he accepts the invitation," Samantha said.

Nikki remembered Axel, the rough boy with an English accent. She had rescued him from the Power Trappers, too, but, unlike Britney, he had decided not to join the Power Council. At first Nikki thought he would join the Power Outlaws, but now she wasn't sure. He was a bit rough around the edges, and could even be mean sometimes, like when he made fun of Freddy being a little bit chubby, but he had also saved the day at the end with his dart gun. All in all, Nikki sort of liked Axel. She hoped he would attend the meeting.

But Spencer wasn't just thinking about Axel. "What about the three unidentified power kids?" he asked. Nikki's head jerked up as she realized what Spencer was getting at. She had recently learned the number of power kids was limited to 12, and that each kid had 12 powers, for a total of 144 powers. So far, they had met nine of them. First, the Power Council and its five power kids; second, the Power Outlaws and its three members; and lastly, Axel, the only known power kid who hadn't joined a side. That left three power kids unaccounted for.

"They would have been invited, too...whoever they are," Samantha said.

The butterflies that lived in Nikki's stomach began to flutter. In just a few minutes she would be meeting the last three power kids! A million questions about them ran through her mind in an instant.

Would they be good kids or bad. Or would they be neutral like Axel? Would they agree to participate in the Great Adventure? What kinds of powers would they have and where would they get their powers from? Were they boys or girls? Nikki hoped girls—she was really getting along well with Samantha and Britney, although she couldn't stand Naomi Powerskirts.

As these questions flooded her head, Nikki found herself marching along beside her friends, as Samantha led them through the Power City. She barely noticed the exquisite tunnels they walked through. One was coated in diamonds and another had beautiful rosebushes along the arch. Soon they reached their destination: the room with the purple couches. The room really didn't have a name, but it had two huge purple, sectional couches, so most of the Power Council just called it the purple couch room. It's where they would hang out, eat meals, and watch the news for any sightings of the Power Outlaws.

Nikki slumped down into the plush couch and Spencer flopped next to her. Three other kids were already sitting on the couch across from them. There were two boys and a girl.

Spencer raised a hand to his head and saluted them. "Well, hello fellow Power Council members," he said very formally.

The girl with the dark black hair and the dark eyes laughed. Her name was Chilly Weathers (no joke). She was Freddy's sidekick and had a knack for magic tricks. The small, Asian boy sitting next to her returned Spencer's salute. His name was Dexter and he served as Samantha's sidekick. He was good with booby traps. Real good.

The third kid—a chubby, dark-skinned boy named Freddy—said, "Mike—where have you been? We're starving here! Bring on lunch I say!"

Nikki hadn't noticed before, but after hearing Freddy she realized her stomach was aching with hunger. Flying was hard work and she always felt extra hungry afterwards. One second the table in between the couches was empty. The next second it was full of food! You see, one of Mike's powers was to create food out of thin air. He could create anything, although mostly the power kids requested junk food, like pizza and burgers. But today was Nikki's turn to make a request, and earlier she had asked Mike to keep it healthy for a change, with fruit and salads and nuts. To her delight the table was full of red, shiny apples, ripe peaches, yellow bananas, big salads with all the fixings, and bowls of peanuts and pistachios.

"Thanks, Mike," Nikki said, as she began preparing a plate. The other kids did the same, and soon they were busily eating. No one complained that the food was healthy. In fact, they all seemed to be enjoying it. Nikki's mom would have been proud!

Once their stomachs were full, Nikki said, "Where are we meeting the rest of the power kids?"

"Not here I hope," Mike said.

Samantha said, "Of course not. As far as we know, the Power City remains a secret and I'd like to keep it that way. No, the meeting place will be somewhere neutral—a place the Weebles are calling the Sands of Destiny."

"The Sands of Destiny?" Spencer said. "What is that supposed to mean?"

Samantha shrugged. "I'm not sure," she said.

"Then how will we get there?" Nikki asked.

"I don't know that either," Samantha said. "But the Weebles seem to think it won't be a problem. Maybe they will lead us there."

"Maybe," Spencer said. He started humming to himself, a sure sign that he was thinking. After a few minutes of silence he said, "The way I see it, there are only three options. One, Samantha is right and the Weebles will lead us to the Sands of Destiny. Two, the power kids will need to use their superpowers to get us all there. Or three, we will travel by powerbracelet."

"Powerbracelet?" Nikki said. She had almost forgotten about her powerbracelet. When she had first found the thin, silver band in the bottom of her powerchest, she was in awe of the simple beauty of the single blue gemstone that adorned it. From time to time the blue jewel would flash brightly, and then drain of all color, revealing a spinning image of a glove inside. The glove would change color, telling her which of her powergloves to put on. As soon as she wore whatever pair of gloves the powerbracelet told her to, she would be transported to wherever her help was needed. She always wore her powerbracelet, although it hadn't flashed for at least two weeks.

Samantha said, "That's an interesting theory, Spencer. You could be right."

"I usually am," Spencer said matter-of-factly. Nikki laughed. Someone who didn't know Spencer would probably think he was full of himself after a comment like that, but she knew he was just smart. Too smart for his own good sometimes, but smart nonetheless.

"I guess we'll just have to wait and see," Samantha said. So they waited. And waited. And then waited some more. It seemed like hours were passing. After a while, Nikki curled up on the big purple couch with her head on Spencer's lap. After flying around all morning, Nikki's eyelids felt heavy. She felt them being tugged downwards by some invisible force, gravity maybe.

Just as they were about to close, the room was lit up by a blinding light. It seemed to shoot in all directions, painting the walls and ceiling with brilliantly colored spotlights. Her head jerked up and suddenly she was wide awake. At first she didn't know where the light beams were coming from and she thought they might be under attack, or perhaps one of her friends was using one of their powers to play a trick on the rest of them, but soon she realized what was causing the light display.

Powerbracelets.

Spencer's guess had been right, as usual. Each kid's powerbracelet was lit up, shooting a different colored beam of light through the air. Nikki looked at her own powerbracelet. Blue light burst from the gem. It was so bright she had to squint to look at it, and even then, she could only gaze at it from the corner of her eye.

Normally, this was the point where the gem would drain of all color, becoming clear and revealing the color of the powerglove that she was supposed to wear. But this time was different. The gem stayed blue. No glove was revealed. *Weird*, she thought.

"Flying butt-monkeys from under the deep, blue sea!" Spencer exclaimed.

"I guess you were right, Spencer," Samantha said.

"What do we do? The Powerbracelets aren't showing us which glove to use," Nikki said.

Mike said, "This happened to me once before." All head's turned to look at Mike. He was grinning, like he was happy to have a secret that only he knew about. He said, "All you have to do is push a thumb to the gemstone and you'll be transported wherever the powerbracelet wants you to go."

"But what about the sidekicks?" Dexter asked.

"You mean you guys don't know—" Samantha started to say, making eye contact with Nikki and then Spencer. Nikki just stared at Samantha; she had no idea what she was talking about. Samantha continued: "I guess not. Well, you can bring your sidekick along whenever you teleport using the powerbracelet. All you have to do is touch him just before you get transported, and he will magically come with you."

"Slap me on the knee and call me Aunt Sally!" Spencer said. Everyone laughed. He was being even funnier than normal.

When the laughing died down, Samantha said, "Is everyone linked to their sidekick?" She already had a hand on Dexter's knee.

Freddy said, "Ready." His hand was on Chilly's shoulder.

Spencer grabbed Nikki's hand and shouted, "Aye, aye, El Capitano!"

Samantha said, "Okay, touch your gems now!"

Nikki jammed her thumb onto the shining blue jewel in her bracelet and everything went black.

A few seconds later everything went white. Nikki looked around. It wasn't that everything was white, just the ground beneath her. And it was soft, too. White and soft. Sandy, like a beach, except she couldn't see or hear the ocean. She was sitting on the ground.

Spencer was sitting next to her, looking around, too. The rest of the Power Council were scattered along the side of the sand dune. It was hot and the sun was beating down on them. Nikki was sweating already and she hadn't even moved.

She gazed into the distance, looking for a landmark, but saw only white, sandy dunes for as far as she could see. She felt someone brush past her and realized that Spencer had stood up and was running down the slope. "Woohoo!" he yelled and then tripped, falling end over end and rolling all the way to the bottom. "Ooch, oww, eek, ooch, yikes!" he yelled as he rolled.

Serves him right for messing around, Nikki thought.

As she watched her brave sidekick pull himself back to his feet and slowly trudge back up the dune covered in sand, she heard a shout from above her, higher up on the hill. It was Freddy. Evidently he had landed at the peak of the slope and could see further than the rest of them. "Over here!" he shouted.

Not bothering to wait for Spencer, Nikki scrambled up the slippery dune. She was the first to reach Freddy's side.

Her stomach dropped when she saw what he was looking at.

A gigantic, round valley was ringed by a circle of dunes, including the one they were standing on. It was as if a meteor had struck the spot, leaving a huge indentation. But that wasn't the most amazing thing. What Nikki was interested in was who was at the bottom of the crater. Hundreds of Weebles were playing in the sand, burying each other, using their arms and legs to create sand angels, building tall, intricately designed sand castles and then smashing them to smithereens.

She recognized one of them, a small, black Weeble named Roy, who had helped them defeat the Power Trappers by introducing her to a gang of friendly gnomes. He saw her, too, and shouted, "Hey, Nikki!"

144

He rolled up the hill to greet her, moving up the soft sand far quicker than a human could walk up it. His spiny bristles left little tracks in the sand.

When he reached the top, he said, "Glad you made it. The Great Weeble is here, too." He pointed a paw to one end of the valley, where a raised platform had been constructed out of sand. The tiniest Weeble of all was alone on the platform. He was bouncing up and down on his butt, laughing his head off like a crazy person…or a crazy Weeble.

Nikki was so excited to see the Weebles that at first she didn't notice who else was in the crater. As she gazed at the festivities, however, she saw them. Seven kids, sitting off to the side, watching the Weebles. There were two groups of three, each sitting a few feet away from each other, and one lone boy, sitting by himself.

Nikki turned to look at Mike and saw that the rest of her friends were standing behind her, taking in everything that she had just seen. "They're here," Nikki said. "All the power kids are here." She tried not to be scared but felt her body trembling a little.

Evidently the fear was showing on her face, because Samantha said, "Don't worry, Nikki. We'll be okay. The Power Outlaws won't be able to do anything to us here. Not with the Weebles around."

Nikki looked at Samantha and saw that her eyes were confident, her mouth firm. Nikki felt better knowing that Samantha was with them. She was a great leader.

Roy led the way down the white sand, rolling out in front of them. Nikki half-slid, half-walked down the crumbly slope. The whole way down she could feel the stares from the Power Outlaws, but avoided eye contact.

The crowd of Weebles at the bottom was so thick that there wasn't even anywhere to stand. The only place to go was back toward where the other power kids were sitting. Nikki glanced up and caught the gaze of Jimmy Powerboots. He glared at her.

Surprising even herself, Nikki glared right back at him. Whenever she was around Jimmy Powerboots she just felt so angry all the time.

He was always trying to do bad stuff, hurt people, destroy things. Now, locked in a staring contest with Jimmy, any fear Nikki had of the Power Outlaws vanished in an instant. She wasn't a scared girl anymore, she was Nikki Powergloves, villain-fighting superhero!

After only ten seconds, Jimmy smirked and looked away from Nikki. *Round one to me,* Nikki thought.

Samantha had watched the silent exchange between Nikki and Jimmy. When it finished, she hesitated for just a moment, and then strode off toward where the power kids were sitting. She ignored Jimmy, Peter, and Naomi as she passed them, and Nikki followed her lead and did the same, pretending they weren't even there. Nikki hoped Spencer would be smart enough to ignore them, too.

He wasn't.

Nikki heard him mumble, "Loser laser," as he passed and then he said, "Bang, bang, bang," as if he were shooting them.

"What did you say to me?" Naomi said. When Spencer didn't answer, she said, "Hey, I'm talkin' to you!"

Nikki whirled around and frowned at Naomi. "Don't talk to my sidekick....ever," Nikki said.

"What are you gonna do about it?" Naomi said. Her eyes were dark and fierce. The Asian girl looked like a ninja warrior from some old karate movie. Nikki glanced at Jimmy, he looked amused. Peter Powerhats was sitting between them, looking like a big, dumb ox. Nikki thought about starting a fight—how good it would feel to knock some sense into the Power Outlaws—but then she thought better of it. If she retaliated, she would be acting just like them. As a superhero, she needed to be better than that. Set a good example.

"Let's go, Spence," she said, grabbing Spencer's hand and pulling him away.

She heard Naomi say, "Aww, is your little sidekick your boyfriend, too?" Nikki ignored her. Now wasn't the time. She caught up with Samantha, who was approaching the other three power kids sitting in a group. The new ones.

In her usual friendly fashion, Samantha went right up to them and introduced herself. "I'm Samantha Powerbelts," she said.

The first kid in the row stuck out a big, black hand. He was huge. The other two kids' faces were hidden by the shadow cast by his body.

"Tyrone Powerbling," he growled.

"The rest of my friends are members of the Power Council," Samantha said, gesturing behind her. As Tyrone looked Nikki up and down, she tried to avoid making direct eye contact with his dark eyes. Instead, she looked at the rest of him.

He had said his name was Tyrone Power*bling*, which meant his powers came from jewelry. The only problem was that he was wearing so much jewelry she couldn't guess which item gave him powers.

A bright gold chain hung from his neck and his ears were capped by big diamond studs. On one wrist was a thick gold watch—it looked expensive. The other wrist had four or five gold bracelets. Hidden beneath them she could just make out the form of his powerbracelet. Like Freddy, he had dark skin, but the similarities ended there. Tyrone was in good shape and had arms and legs that looked like those of a teenager, although she knew he was only nine years old, like the rest of the power kids.

"It's nice to meet you," Tyrone said in the deepest voice Nikki had ever heard. He didn't sound like he meant it.

Nikki mumbled, "You, too."

Samantha had already moved on to the next kid, who had shifted her position so that her face moved out of Tyrone's shadow. Nikki's breath caught when she saw her face. The girl was beautiful, like a doll. She had shimmering blond hair that fell well beyond her shoulders. Her eyes were a captivating green hue that seemed to draw Nikki's eyes to her. She was smiling a perfect smile. But Nikki could tell it wasn't genuine. It looked like the smile of the beauty pageant girls that Nikki had seen on TV. The girl was only smiling because she felt she had to. Behind the smile was a girl who wished she didn't have to smile.

"I'm Sue Powerslippers," she said sweetly, taking Samantha's hand first, and then Nikki's. The girl's hand felt icy, like her skin and bones had been chilled in the freezer. Right away, Nikki didn't like her. She was the exact opposite of Samantha, who was always genuine. Nikki glanced down and saw the girl's slippers, the source of her power. They were pink ballet slippers. Nikki wondered what the girl could do with them.

The last girl was less beautiful. And that was putting it nicely. This girl had clearly fallen out of the ugly tree and hit every branch on the way down. She had knotted black hair and a crooked nose. Her eyes were crossed, and her lips and cheeks sagged in a perpetual frown. And yet, Nikki already liked her more than Sue, who looked practically perfect in every way.

"Tanya Powershirts," the girl mumbled. Nikki hadn't even noticed her shirt, but now she checked it out. Tanya was wearing a plain black t-shirt with a white skeleton on it.

Nikki realized she was still staring at the bones when Tanya sneered, "Can I help you?"

"Uh, no, sorry," Nikki stammered. She moved past Tanya quickly, catching up to Samantha, who had sat down in the sand. Nikki's face lit up when she saw who Samantha had sat next to.

"Axel!" she exclaimed.

Axel Powerjackets looked at her strangely and Nikki realized how odd her reaction had been. For one, she barely even knew Axel. She had only met him once, and although they had fought alongside each other to defeat the Power Trappers, he hadn't been particularly nice to her. And he was downright mean to Freddy, making fun of him being kinda fat. There was no real reason she should be so happy to see him. And yet she was. Maybe it was because she had just walked past six kids who seemed even meaner. Or maybe there was something about Axel that she just liked.

Nikki said, "Uh, how are you, Axel?"

In his smooth English accent, Axel said, "Terrible. I'm stuck here, aren't I?"

Nikki's face fell. She was hoping he would say something nicer. She didn't reply. Instead, she sat down, keeping Samantha between her and Axel. The rest of her friends crowded up behind them on the dunes. Spencer sat right next to her. He was the only one smiling. It seemed seeing the other power kids had brought all their moods down. But not Spencer's. He was excited, watching the Weebles and turning his head to stare at the new power kids.

"Isn't it awesome?" he said.

"What?" Nikki asked curiously.

"All the power kids in one place at the same time. Pretty cool, huh, Nikki McPowergloves?"

Nikki hadn't thought about it like that. Spencer always had a way of shedding things in a positive light. It *was* pretty cool, as Spencer had said. Twelve power kids. Twelve powers each. Ready to do battle.

Made in the USA
Middletown, DE
11 June 2015